SOMBRIO

a novel by
RHONDA WATERFALL

Edited by Jeremy Luke Hill
Cover and book design by Jeremy Luke Hill
Proofread by Carol Dilworth
Set in Linux Libertine
Printed on Mohawk Via Felt
Printed and bound by Arkay Design & Print

LIBRARY AND ARCHIVES CANADA CATALOGUING IN PUBLICATION

Title: Sombrio / a novel by Rhonda Waterfall.
Names: Waterfall, Rhonda, 1973- author.
Identifiers: Canadiana (print) 2022024684X | Canadiana (ebook) 20220246866 |
    ISBN 9781774220672 (softcover) | ISBN 9781774220689 (PDF) |
    ISBN 9781774220696 (HTML)
Classification: LCC PS8645.A837 S66 2022 | DDC C813/.6—dc23

ONTARIO ARTS COUNCIL
CONSEIL DES ARTS DE L'ONTARIO
an Ontario government agency
un organisme du gouvernement de l'Ontario

Gordon Hill Press gratefully acknowledges the support of the Ontario Arts Council.

Gordon Hill Press respectfully acknowledges the ancestral homelands of the Attawandaron, Anishinaabe, Haudenosaunee, and Métis Peoples, and recognizes that we are situated on Treaty 3 territory, the traditional territory of Mississaugas of the Credit First Nation.

Gordon Hill Press also recognizes and supports the diverse persons who make up its community, regardless of race, age, culture, ability, ethnicity, nationality, gender identity and expression, sexual orientation, marital status, religious affiliation, and socioeconomic status.

Gordon Hill Press
130 Dublin Street North
Guelph, Ontario, Canada
N1H 4N4
www.gordonhillpress.com

A story as true as any

THOMAS DEWOLF

"Words are loneliness."
— Henry Miller

We've been here now for a week, in these moss soaked woods, hidden away from the chaos that will erupt as soon as the hands of old Father Time tick tock into the new year. Outside our door, waves crash onto the grey rocks of Sombrio Beach in an endless clamour. Damp worms through the shingles and earthen floor of our ramshackle shelter. This shelter, which we've commandeered, was not too long ago abandoned by squatters. Squatters who didn't leave on their own accord but were forced off the land by the provincial government, even though they caused no harm, conjured vegetable gardens from this acidic soil, and in peace raised feral children under the shade of the giant Sitka spruce and hemlock trees. Now we're the squatters, so far undetected by the authorities. We've reinforced the shelter with beach debris, plywood, sheet metal, and hope. Hope most of all, for we've gone back to the land.

I'm here with two others, Charles and Roy. Charles is a master artist of staggering skill and vision. His talent has always been a wonder to me, in all the many, many years we've been friends. Roy may be a lost cause, but I suppose no more than the rest of us. There's a kernel of Roy that fills me with unease and reminds me of myself as a boy. My wife visits when my drug supply runs low. Fern, Roy's girlfriend, visits too, keeping our cold-box and shelves stocked with food. We're all here for our own reasons, but I can only speak of my own. I need to clear my head, then return to the outside world and be a proper father to my daughter, Iris. If she'll allow me. I wouldn't blame her if she

1

didn't want me in her life. Twenty years I've failed her. I failed her even before she was birthed into the world. The genesis of the failures that would be unleashed in her life started to take root in my very own conception. This only goes to prove that my beautiful daughter has no faults. Her sadness, her addictions, her brokenness, all the blame rests at my feet. Everything. Iris.

I've used every day since we arrived. The plan was to quit the drugs when we got to Sombrio, but to quit, it seems, is something that can always be done tomorrow. Every fix is the last one, as has always been the case. I go to my own damp corner of the shelter, inoculate myself and want nothing more from the day than for the light to grow, peak, and then fade into a dark and hollow emptiness. My thoughts distant with only a numb static that reverberates in my brain to prove I am alive. Perhaps we can stay here forever. We're only a month from knowing if the world ends or not, for what it's worth.

ROY KRUK

"Great geniuses always produce mediocre children."
— Salvador Dali

Fern should be the first word out of every mouth. Fern. What can I say: you're everything that pulses within me. You're my very marrow. You're my moth mate. Much of what I document here will be nothing new to you, Fern, but it will answer everything for those in a future place—academics, art critics, historians, and the like. Everything has been transcribed in triplicate: one version for you, one version held by me, and a third I will bury in a steel box in this forest where we have come for salvation. The buried box for excavation in some unknown future world, to be unearthed like a clay pot in Pompeii.

I braid my hair in two ropes that hang down my back, the ends dipped in sandalwood oil and tied off with red string. Remember how you poked them the night I met you, in that basement bar, and you asked if I was going to a pow-wow. Then you laughed, a real laugh, an unhinged laugh that I knew would wrap itself around my neck and not let go. I imagine myself to be a majestic man on the edge of the western frontier, about to ride a horse into Indian Territory to fight alongside the Iron Confederacy. On my chest, a tattoo of a circle with a cross at its centre in the form of a plus sign, that symbolizes fire. This is our life experience, one big circle with a fire in the middle that will not stop burning. All we can do is tend the flames, to prevent an inferno that takes everything away.

I was born in a small inland town on Vancouver Island. My mother's people were a jumble of Western Europeans so far back no one can name the places they originated from. On my father's side, they came from Russia, supposedly near the Ural Mountains. But what does that mean? For dinners, we ate boiled wieners, carrots, canned peas, along with white bread and mustard sandwiches. When mom was distracted, we stole cups of white flour to eat in the woods, a gooey paste formed on our tongues and the roof of our mouths. There were six of us, me, and my siblings. We would kick the feet out from one another for an extra piece of liver.

You, Fern, say none of this shit matters: where we come from, what our childhoods were like. You might be right, but then you had none of these experiences. You had two parents who lived together, who didn't want to kill each other. You were fed on a regular basis. You say people need to rise above their pasts, but you didn't have to rise above anything. Your past lifts you up like a gold-plated escalator toward all that is good and true in this world.

My escalator only goes to the cottage on the lake and a headdress of eagle feathers worn by a fat white man. A lake tainted yellow by the cedar stumps that rot on its boggy floor. Why the headdress? Can you imagine being haunted by something you have no explanation for? Now, when I see a headdress I am suddenly nine-years-old with gangly limbs, a badly shorn head, dark circles under my eyes, and an empty belly, like some kid stumbling out of a Nazi concentration camp. Every moment of my life, I am that kid, alone in a broke-down cottage with light breaking through the dirty plate-glass window. I imagine that light to be sharp, to cut me in half, or to be a bomb, a bomb of light, that detonates and sends shattered glass through the air to slice throats and detach limbs. The dark forest floor left littered with timber and small-boy parts. How my forty-year-old self smiles at the image of my dead nine-year-old self, my blood seeping into the forest bed of pine needles and horsetail roots. There's more than one way to be immortal—immortal, like Picasso in an Indian headdress.

The day I stepped into the dark forest of Sombrio was the happiest of my life. It was the first time I had a sense that I was about to do something right and essential. I knew in here, I would find what I had always sought, above relief from my mind, more than just an escape, but transcendence. I will become a legend.

I smoke a joint but it doesn't feel like enough; I'll need a drink too. I have no booze, but I know there must be some around. Thomas, after all, is a drunk and a junkie. He thinks he hides it, but everyone knows. Perhaps the only one who doesn't know is Thomas, poor fucking Thomas. He's a poet and an ex-bank robber, if one can be an ex-bank robber. I think what he writes is all right, but Charles thinks it's all shit. Who cares what Charles thinks, anyway. The great master painter that he is or thinks he is, constantly spouting off about his masterwork that takes up one wall of our shack; his Guernica, he calls it. He's so full of himself. I'm his apprentice, but there's nothing he can teach me that I didn't learn before I dropped out of Emily Carr Institute of Art and Design. I rummage through all the hiding spots and find a bottle of Johnnie Walker. Just a drink or two, I say, but I know I'll finish the whole bottle, because I'm thirsty, always so thirsty.

CHARLES TINDAL

"Was I a man or was I a jerk?"
— Saul Bellow

I know where that heifer Fern is at all times. I can sense her as she skulks through the woods. I can smell her as she lounges about like some puss, inert on a sun-soaked window sill. All she does is take up space. She adds nothing to the conversation and carries no intellectual depth. She is all show, fawn eyes, and long twenty-something legs. Her sketchbook is filled with twee, juvenile attempts at what I don't know. Before we leave this dank forest, I'll have my way with her.

Although, it's thanks in part to Fern that we are here at Sombrio. She's the one who suggested the location for our exit from society. We were all at my James Bay studio in Victoria, not too long ago: Thomas a junkie and ex-bank robber, Roy my weasel of an apprentice, and Fern his child-like chattel. Thomas, of course, was strung out, his pockets stuffed with drugs. He's like a steel drum with a hole at its bottom. He can never be full. The worst of it is that he fancies himself a poet, but what he writes is garbled nonsense. Every once in a while, his ink-stained fingers reach for a dog-eared pad of paper and he scratches something out. But that night, at my studio, Thomas fixed and shot drugs into his arm, right in front of us, which I felt showed a certain amount of slovenliness and stupidity for an ex-bank robber. Then he rolled onto his back and closed his eyes. Roy started to talk about how the financial system was going to crash and the government would seize full control.

"They've been tracking us for years, waiting for this," he blabbered.

Thomas sat up and snorted. "They always round up the artists first." Then he took out his sad little pad of paper and pencilled a few lines.

"Thomas," I said, "read to us what greatness you have scribbled on your tablet."

He blinked at us as if I had spoken some foreign language.

"Stand," Roy called out.

"Yes, stand," Fern echoed.

Thomas blinked again and then pushed himself to his feet.

The Prairie
Dust in my mouth
Hot metal
Fall Fall Fall
Thunderhead
Dust in my mouth
Dust in my lungs
Pressing down
The heat
Branded X

When he stopped, his arms fell to his side, the little pad hit his thigh.

"Is that all?" I asked.

Fern jumped up and started to clap like some small-town cheerleader. "Did you write that today?" she yelped. "Genius," she added. I wish she wouldn't encourage him.

Roy gave a few claps. "Fuck ya," he hollered, as if it was the grandest thing he had ever heard.

Thomas collapsed onto a cushion, depleted, and began to finger through a handful of pills he dug from his pocket. For the rest of the night he was as quiet as a sullen puppy. Roy prattled on about the new year. How airplanes were going to fall out of the sky. Riots would cause chaos, stores would be looted.

Ideas started to stir in my head, and then at some point during this sad affair it occurred to me what we needed to do. We needed to leave this fetid neighbourhood with its stain of domesticity, the school children who tromped past my studio, morning and afternoon, with their shrill voices. The cafés packed with yoga pant clad drones, their plump bottoms parked in our chairs. The latte guzzlers with their bug-eyed infants. We couldn't become great amongst the albatross of picket fences, family vans, and running shoes. "We must find a place to hide," I announced to the gathered. "We must leave to reach the pinnacle of greatness, to rise above the doldrums of this society."

Fern, who thinks quicker than the rest and has not blunted herself with drug and drink like the others, was enthusiastic. "I know where we should go," she called out.

I didn't ask her to elucidate. After all, this plan wasn't meant to include her. No broads wanted on the boat, I would say.

Fern turned to Roy, hit him on the arm to bring him out of whatever daydream was behind his dumb expression.

"Sombrio," she said to him.

"What?" he said.

"Sombrio, the squatter community."

"That's no longer there."

"Right."

Roy's eyes opened wide. "That's it, Fern has it," he said. "Sombrio."

THOMAS

Somehow, Charles, a real pied piper, has scraped-up a dozen women who trek through the woods in their glittery attire. The chafed spikes of their high-heeled shoes, pierce the old-growth loam and sap from the rough bark of ancient trees, soils their pretty hands. They arrive invigorated and awed at what they stumble into. The shelter's interior is lit with the flicker and glow of tea lights. On a battered transistor radio the CBC plays John Coltrane. The women swish their long hair and sway their bodies. We all smoke hash and drink and dance. The women laugh, unaware that they too are dying.

One of the women, her words a slurry mess asks, "Why are you out here?" She chortles as if what she has asked is funny.

"We're waiting for the end of the world," I say.

"What?" she cackles and sways to one side. The strap of her shimmery dress slips off a shoulder.

"The world is going to end at New Years," I repeat.

"Oh my god," she laughs. "You're kidding."

—

I retreat and sulk in my dark corner, wanting to ride out my gloomy high in peace. My brain wants to do everything and nothing. A vast wave of hate washes over me. Violent thoughts bounce around inside my head, blood splattered walls, broken glass. I do what I can to push the thoughts away. I am, I am, is the mantra I repeat over and over to myself. Then a sweet angel, like a young Aphrodite comes over to visit me in my glum hide-away. The smell of apricot and new earth on her skin. She approaches me as if I'm someone safe to approach. If only she knew what was inside my brain, how my hands want to squeeze life until there is none. Can you imagine these girls who give

9

away their love so freely, their garments made of gold leaf that dissolves under the warmth of a man's touch. Can you imagine a man being this way, just loving, no ill will, no dark thoughts, just open free love? No wonder women live longer. Their hearts go untarnished, no matter.

She wants to know what it's like to rob a bank. Her plump lips are close to mine. How she is privy to my past occupation, I don't know. And why do they always ask what it's like to rob a bank? Why not ask what it's like to ruin everything I've ever loved? Why not ask what it's like to be violated as a child or to just want to die? But no, it's always the bank robbing question. I tell her what I tell every woman—it was fucking magnificent. She's heard everything she needs to hear, and her lips are on mine. She makes love to me as if I am her equal with the Lord's dim light upon us. Then, as if resurrected, I'm alive, and we dance out on the dirt-stained Persian rug and drink messy cupfuls of gin. For a moment, I forget my deep-deep misery.

Soon my bones begin to ache, and I sit on one of the floor pillows, off to the side, against the wall. It is then I notice Fern. She leans against one of the tree trunks that support our shelter. She has a drink in one hand, but I can tell she is sober as a rock. Cooly, she observes the gathered circus. What her thoughts are I don't know. Across the room, Roy, her partner, is in the midst of a tangle of women. The women fawn over him as he extols his talents with great vigour. He shows them his sketches of nude women and draws intricate designs on their faces with silver ink. The women chirp and giggle.

What Fern might see in Roy mystifies me to no end. I fail to understand what an alcoholic, no-account artist's apprentice has to offer. But then I could say the same about myself in regards to my wife. The plasticity of the female heart is boundless. Fern, with her drink, heads to the door and in a blink is gone into what must be the fresh forest night. Then I spot Charles, who also has his beady eyes on the door. He slips past the harem of women, and then he too is through the door and out into the night. Part of me wants to follow, see what mischief could be under way, but why. Let people do what they want. Who am I to get involved? To be abandoned with my thoughts and sleep is all I want.

In a dream, I hear crying. The sound leads me outside and to my daughter. She's folded forward from the hips and recites something over and over, but the words make no sense. I step closer to her, and she stands up, her mouth shaped as if she is in mid scream, but no sound emerges. She is so much of me, same eyes, same brow, and cheek bones. All her damage done at my hands, done with my absence and neglect. I step still closer to her and see that she is covered in blood. With her bare hands, she has torn into her gut; skin and muscle hang in tattered strips. She reaches into the red mush and pulls out a blue-skinned, still infant. I wake soaked in sweat, sick to my stomach, a scream lodged in my throat.

Women slumber, spread out on the floor, like starfish, clinging to any surface that holds comfort. Roy sleeps intertwined in the limbs of a woman, her large breasts white and exposed. I get up and leave the shelter for the crisp morning air of the forest, the land still damp from the night. I retch up the vile contents of my insides and go down to the beach to sit on the sand.

The ocean is vast and hungry. It asks nothing of you and cares nothing for your life. For a moment we commune, and I breathe in its mist and metal, with its endless emptiness. I place my cheek against the cold sand and hope for the waves to crush me. It's the longer trail that I take back toward the shelter, the one that trickles along just inside the tree line. The forest is so still and peaceful, the light soft with a smudge of blush on the watery horizon. At times like this I can hardly believe we exist here on this earth. It fills me with self loathing. Why do I even get to enjoy it, when so many others can't? The older I get, the more my world is filled with the ghosts of dead friends.

The trail sweeps back toward the shelter and up over a small rise. On the other side, in a hollow beside a fallen cedar, lie Fern and another woman. Their bodies wrapped around each other, covered in a white cape, eyes closed, fast asleep like lambs. At first I think this must be one of the women from the party, but on longer study I don't believe she is. There's something faintly familiar about her, and it's not until I get back to the shelter and see Charles that I know the woman is Charles' daughter, the youngest one of his three, Cedar.

ROY

Women are like parasites, suckling babes who bleed you of everything you have and leave you a dried up husk. At the party, they gather around me to be sketched. They want so much to see themselves reflected on paper, to see themselves beautiful, their souls read like a fortune-teller reads the leaves on the bottom of a teacup.

I tell them about Lucian Freud, a painter over there in England. How he painted portraits of women who orbited in his life. Women who were renowned for their beauty, but in Freud's portraits often their faces would be dark and pinched with thick gashes of paint. You would know you were seeing their insides, their spirit, and their soul. The dark recesses of their needy minds and the haunted corners of their sad hearts. I wrote him a letter once but I never heard back.

Dear Mr Freud

You are a genius. We have much in common. I would like to come to England and work with you. What do you think? I believe we would get on like best compadres. I could carry on your legacy. Give it some thought. I have included a sketch at the bottom to give you an idea of my skills. I studied at Emily Carr for a year but they were jackasses and I left. Genius needs no school, only paint, canvas, and space, as I am sure you would agree.

Best
Roy Kruk

What was it you said, Fern, when you saw Freud's most recent work? Maybe he is just getting old and sloppy. Such a Fern thing to say. Your simplicity entertains me.

"Great artists do not get old and sloppy," I said.

"Picasso did," you came back with.

You are like a field of wildflowers I want to mow or douse with gasoline and set ablaze.

The party women all press in, and I feel the tide turn. At some point they will reveal their dark wounded hearts. And I will want to cut those hearts out of their birdcage chests. Set the bitches free, I say. I can always sense the early stages of evil's bloom. When my son, Shane, was born, I could see it in him, under the yellow light of the operating theatre. The doc asked if I wanted to hold him. No, I thought, he's not my son but an imposter. I looked down at his mother, drenched in sweat on the table, and I saw in her eyes too, the hardening of her heart, the bloom of evil.

But tonight it's these women—whom Charles has somehow rounded up and brought out here to our shack—who hold my attention. They want to see my drawings and sketches, and I'm more than happy to show them. They flatter me with their words, and although I know they're all uneducated opinions from empty minds, I'm nonetheless drawn to their nectar. I focus in on one; she has wild hair and a plumpness about her that I find alluring. The others can sense how she's gained my selective attention, and they turn sour; their little mouths purse and their eyes drop. They dig their fingernails into the Persian rug. I reach out and touch the chain of little beads that the wild-haired one wears around her neck. She tips her head to one side and tells me she got the necklace in Tofino. Her eyes grow big, and I plunge my hands into her hair. How amazing that at these moments I can be so filled with love and rage at the same time. Always I have to tamp one down like embers that have leapt from a fire. I sink my face between her breasts. There is no more comforting place.

CHARLES

I filled this hovel with broads. I left the woods and rounded them up myself. Roy and Thomas couldn't round up their own thoughts let alone some women for a good time. Have they thanked me? No. Do they think these women appeared on their own? Sniffed their own way through the woods like sows rooting for truffles? No. I went out, and I got them. I'm the one who lured them with my intellect. Even the dumbest broad is turned on by the spark of original thought. It stirs something in them that I'm sure they would struggle to articulate with language. This is one of the faults of women—they cannot bother to strive for the highest of pursuits on their own, but they will damn well marry it as quick as they can.

I told the women about my masterpiece. How I came to the woods to be away from distraction and from the common masses who will pillage as soon as the world implodes in the new year. And to be away from people who want to chew up my time and attention. Plasma stealers, my old friend William Burroughs would say. The canvas takes up one entire wall inside the hovel. All I do is bore into it with my mind and wait for it to talk to me, to tell me what it wants. This painting will be my *Guernica*, my *Seagram Mural*, my *Last Supper*. Of course these women needed to see it.

I brought these women like Zeus brings lightning, and now Roy has his metaphorical cock out, stroking it for display to the gathered hens. They all cluck at him like he's something special. They fawn over his weak talents, smudged charcoal on discount paper. The same sketches he tires everyone with. With their soft lines and poorly articulated expressions, they lack any originality. These broads really are dumb.

Fern seems to have taken a back seat tonight. She wanders in the periphery and lurks in the shadows. She observes her pathetic "partner" as she calls him. Partner. What goes on in her head? Who knows. And Thomas, I see him over there in his corner, busy getting his ego nursed by some vacant flower child.

I observe Fern take her exit, slipping out into the night. Here's my opportunity. I follow her and track her through the trees. Her footfalls are light, like an animal, like a deer. No sound. She stops and so do I. She tilts her head to the side. Does she hear something? Me? Does she sense something in the air? She takes another step. I take a step, and there's the sharp crack of a branch under my foot. She turns and scans the terrain she has covered.

"Darling?" she says.

Darling? Who could that be? "No, Charles," I say.

"Oh, what are you doing?"

"What are *you* doing?" I ask her. Perhaps I have caught her hands near the cookie jar.

"Fresh air," she says.

We recline in the mossy dip of two western hemlock trees. The stars are bright between breaks in the canopy.

"The air this night feels like the air one particular evening in Paris," I say. "When I started one of my masterpieces, titled *Full Moon*. A painting that now resides in the National Gallery of Canada."

She has no response for this and remains silent.

"My painting in the National Gallery is hung beside a Tom Thomson," I say. Again, she cannot seem to conjure up a response.

"I don't know who that is," she says.

So many times I want to strangle her. The things that come out of her mouth. She twirls a twig in her hand and strips the bark off with a thumbnail.

"Where's the National Gallery?" she asks.

"Ottawa."

"Have you been there?"

"No," I say.

"Sounds like an awful place anyway. Ottawa, that is, not the National Gallery."

"May very well be. What place would you find more compelling?" I ask her.

"Right here," she says. "Doesn't it feel as if all the energies of the earth are bending down right here where we are?"

Christ, her brain is full of granola and hemp.

"Your profile looks magnificent in the moonlight. I should paint you," I say.

"Sure," she responds with complete disinterest. "Are you trying to make some pathetic move on me?"

She's such a wet blanket. Everything about her deflates me. "Yes, and you should become pregnant."

"You've got to be kidding," she laughs.

"There is nothing more beautiful than the pregnant form."

"What about the child though?"

"We would raise it together."

"But you already have three daughters you never raised," she says.

Jesus, she wears me out. "Yes, but we, you and I, would be different."

"I'm sure. Besides, girls don't get knocked up any more. Why would I let you slow me down?"

I want to smother her face into the dirt.

She gazes up the tree trunk nearest to us. "I saw a Van Gogh once," she says.

Where this comes from I have no idea, but I nod and say, "That's great." Van Gogh is overrated.

"His paintings are alive. You know what I mean, they move," she says.

"Sure," I say and have grown so tired by this back and forth that I just come out and ask her if we're going to fuck or not.

"Sure," she says and starts to undress.

I cannot stand the blasé commonness of girls these days. Even the way she takes off her clothes irritates me. I take liberties with her body and drink up the youngness under my hands, but ultimately the experience is wholly unsatisfactory to me for reasons I cannot put my finger on, for reasons other than my manhood not being fully up to the task. There's something that irritates me in her ability to flip flop from attentive to detached.

"Where are your thoughts?" I say.

"Oh," she says. "Do you think by living on this land we internalize the past atrocities that have taken place here?"

I wish I never asked. Her eyes are sometimes pretty, but her mouth is ugly. "No," I say.

"But don't you think we hold some responsibility for what our forebears did to the native people?" she says.

"No," I say. "They should buck up. We're the reason they have roads, electricity."

She pops her head through the neck of her sweater like some chipper gopher and then sighs. "When Captain Vancouver came here, he said that all this place needed was to be enriched by the industry of man. As if the men already here had not enriched it."

"They probably hadn't," I say, so tired of this dull conversation. I long to change the subject. "Have you been with Thomas?" I ask.

"No. Why?"

"I can only respect you for not sleeping with that junkie. The bank robber, women can't resist. And Roy, tell me, are his sexual abilities so powerful?"

"Yes," she bluntly states.

"What is it he does? What tricks?"

"Why would I tell you?"

There is a sound in the woods and I shush Fern. "Can you hear that?" I say. "Singing."

We sit in silence for a moment.

"Yes, yes," Fern says. "I hear something. It must be coming from the hideout?"

"No, it's from out there in the dark. I know it's them," I say.

"Who?" she asks.

"My daughters. They have come to slaughter me. I know it."

"What? You're crazy. Why would they do that?"

"Because I am a man and a genius, and they want to engulf me just like their mothers tried." I lean toward the deep of the forest. "It sounds like they are singing *California Dreaming*, that wretched Mamas and the Papas song."

"If you say so," Fern mumbles.

"Jesus, what a racket." I get up and yell into the night, "Shut up, shut up. Enough."

"Your daughters probably just want to talk to you," Fern adds.

"But why?"

"Because you're their dad," she says and shakes her head like I'm the idiot.

"No, they must want something."

"Suit yourself," she says. "I'm leaving the woods tonight. Who wants to see this mess in the daylight. Tell Roy I'll be back in a few days."

Tell him yourself, I think. I'm not her messenger.

"You should ask your daughters how they've been," she says. "When was the last time you saw them?"

"I know they band together," I say.

When Fern is gone, the singing gets louder. Soon it's as if it surrounds me. Perhaps my daughters, by some witchcraft, have diffused themselves into the very air itself so that I might breathe them in and they can kill me from the inside, hatchet away at my lungs, butcher my guts.

"Miranda," I call out. "Miranda." She's my oldest and I assume has gathered her two half sisters for this hunt. "Blue, Cedar," I call out. "Do not listen to your sister. She has led you astray." The singing begins to grow distant, and I step deeper into the woods but then think twice. I'm sure this is their plan, to lure me into the deep forest and do away with me. For a few meters, I follow the sounds of their voices, and I'm sure I see them—Miranda, Blue and Cedar, in long white gowns, like angels or phantoms. And still they sing *California Dreaming*.

"Why do you sing that song?" I yell into the dark.

But the voices fade, and I'm left with the sound of the waves on the beach below and the wind in the trees.

"Damn you. Why would you leave your father in the woods? I am an old man!" I yell but don't expect a response. They have no respect for their father.

ROY

Charles is like an old goat—something dug up from the past with riddles and antiquated words on his tongue. It's a cosmic joke that I'm his apprentice. There's nothing he can teach me. Deep down he believes none of this can be taught anyway, that mastery and genius is either in you at birth or not. Perhaps this is the only thing we agree on.

The big story he uses, to try and impress anyone who will listen, is how he has a painting in the National Gallery of Canada, hung beside a Tom Thomson. When I'm at my meanest, I say this has been done only to illustrate how weak Charles' own technique is, a show of best and worst in the realm of Canadian art. I couldn't tell you what either painting looks like, nor do I give a shit. Many forgotten artists have hung in galleries. But this is the first thing he told me when we met at a café, where I had gone to hide from my wife and infant son.

One of the reasons I claimed you Fern, is because of how you reacted to Charles the first time you met him. You took in his paintings without comment, with no words of praise. He can't handle silence from a woman. It works on his little troll of a soul. He tried to charm you with his stories of palling around with the beats in San Francisco, how close he was to Jack Kerouac.

"Wasn't he a drunk and a loser?" you said.

Fuck, I nearly killed myself laughing. How the gleam in Charles' eyes darkened. Then you turned to study one of his paintings and, unprompted, said, "I like Jack Shadbolt better." Ah, man I would give anything to watch the look on Charles' face again. He shut right up. A discussion was not what he wanted from you. He wanted to dazzle you without confrontation, without inquiry. He wanted praise. But you, Fern, didn't give him that. Fucking magic.

Without your worship, it made it harder for him to go onto his sob story of how his older brother was killed in World War II, and how his father didn't love him, and all that shit.

I tell Charles often that he will die before me—he's practically eighty, nearly double my age— and I'll spend what is left of my own life smearing his legacy. I might even tell people I was the one who actually painted his paintings or that we were lovers. He's from a generation where such a slight would damage his manhood. Perhaps that's all too cruel, but it gives me a kick.

For hours he stares at his painting and does nothing, just ruminates on whatever is in his head. He smokes cigarettes and curses to himself under his breath. The name of his great offering to the world changes every day. If he spots me paying him attention he'll launch into some long drawn out tutorial on how to create a revolutionary work of art. He'll say something goofy like, it must encapsulate the world. Which is funny, because the world as far as we know won't last much longer. Let the slobs in the cities duke it out when the clock sloughs over to the new year. If anyone will survive, it's we in the woods. We'll subsist on roots and berries.

Charles believes his painting will be the only thing to survive and some future civilized people will be raised on his creations. He can really talk some shit sometimes. I tell him they'll replicate his painting and put it on their coffee mugs. He said he might even leave instructions on how to view it, like it's a fucking Pollock or Rothko. Today, he's titled his masterpiece, The 20th Century, as if to present future people with all the fucking awesomeness they missed. At the moment, it's all just black lines, a bunch of bullshit. Except in one corner where there's a woman's face. Almost every goddamn painting he does has this woman in it. I think he only knows how to paint one woman.

"Hey, is that your mother?" I say.

"No, yours," he says. "After I satisfied her."

THOMAS

Fern arrives with groceries and restocks our shelves. Charles and Roy have gone out somewhere, together or separate, I don't know. I ask Fern if she wants to go to the tide pools. Down from where the shelter is, on the beach, there are hollows in the rocks, filled with salt water, warmed, some days, by the sun. Fern and I slip into one of the pools and rest our backs against the hard stone. The view is of a limitless ocean. We've already scavenged most of what there was to eat from the pools—small fish, sea urchin, and other creatures. The tides and winter storms will wash life back into the pools, but for now they're clear for us, as if we're the masters of this land. Fern pulls out two cans of beer and hands me one. She lights a cigarette, and we sit in silence.

"What's up between you and Charles?" I say.

"Nothing," she says.

"I doubt that."

"Nothing worth going on about."

"Would Roy think that?"

"Who cares what Roy thinks," she says. "We're not getting married."

"Why are you with him then?" I say.

"Have you married every girl you been with?" she says.

"I guess not."

"Didn't think so," she says and drinks her beer. "You true to your wife?"

I know she knows the answer to this. "My spirit is true," I say.

"Ha," she says. "My spirit, that's a good one. My spirit is true to many things." She submerges herself. When she pops back up, she slicks back her hair and scrapes the water off with her hands.

"What do you see in Roy?" I ask her.

She takes a drink of her beer. "Entertainment," she says. "And love. But sometimes he's too much. He asks for everything and doesn't offer much in return. He's got issues."

"We've all got issues," I say and laugh.

"Ya, sure. But there's something about Roy. I think deep down he's really disturbed. Like some type of psychosis. Look, I'm not any doctor, but I think there's something truly cracked about him."

"Then why are you fucking him?"

She dips her palm into the pool and watches the water trickle out from between her fingers and melt back into the surface. "I don't know," she says. "I can't break away. I have an unrealistic hope about him."

"A hope for what?"

"You know, that he'll be normal, that we'll spend a life together, he'll be a great artist and I'll be his muse. And we'll have this fantastically bohemian existence. Light, laughter, love and all that shit," she says.

"And Charles?"

"Nothing. Just messing around," she says. "He's gross anyway. He's like some relic, from another time, floating around the ocean. He thinks he's Hemingway or some bullshit."

"And Cedar?" I say.

At this she tips her head back and laughs. "Oh my god, you know everything," she says. "Cedar is lovely. I've known her for years."

"You sleeping with her?" I ask.

"Of course, why not?" she says.

For a while we are in silence, and I can't help but think of my daughter. After all, Fern and Iris are close in age. I wonder if Iris is somewhere having a similar conversation with someone else. I wish it was us together, Iris and me. The thought pains me so deeply I could cry. I feel my face grow hot. I ask Fern if she has another beer and cigarette, and she does.

"What are you going to do when you leave?" she says.

"Sombrio?" I ask although it must be what she is talking about.

"Ya, Sombrio, after New Years."

I take a mouthful of beer and my thoughts go blank. I don't know what I am going to do.

"What's your dream?" she presses. "Your perfect scenario?"

I think hard for a moment, saddened by how dull my dream is. "I just want to live in a cabin in the woods with my wife and daughter."

"That's it?" she says.

"Ya, that's it," I say. "And we would all be clean, you know. And maybe the cabin would be in Costa Rica."

"Do you think the world is going to fall apart on New Years?" she asks.

"The world's already fallen apart," I say and then ask her what she is going to do after.

"I don't know, travel, do stuff. Go back to school."

"Our dreams are so ordinary," I say.

She laughs, "We're just ordinary people."

CHARLES

Roy asks me if I want to go out to the beach. No. I've seen the beach before. I've seen beaches all over the world. I have no need to see this one again. He can go down there if he wants and see what he gets out of it. He should know not to bother me by now. I have greatness to feed. Roy wouldn't understand the significance of what I am doing. How this canvas will become something studied throughout the world. Every stroke will be dismantled and books written about my intentions. I set the undercoat for three forms and give them faces like the devil.

Roy buries his dumb, blank face in his sketchbook, probably drawing a study of what I've set on my canvas. Already they copy me. Roy's mind is empty. He wouldn't understand the struggle needed to create transformative art. After all, I am the one with a painting in the National Gallery, not him, with his soft little sketches of trees and rocks. He's oblivious to my dominance over his girl. It tempts me to tell him what happened just to see the look on his face. But for now I want to savour the victory and recall its deliciousness.

An old friend comes to my mind from San Francisco. Jack, and all those sloths who hung around, puffed up with so much import. They filled dim little rooms with their words. Writers are the dullest bunch. They snap their dry fingers over how a verb has been used in some way that delights them. Honestly, the saddest bunch you can imagine. Their girls with their long-damp hair, who hang on every word. I took every girl Jack ever eyed. Those broads had no idea what hit them. I would turn them right off poetry, right off words on paper.

I take a brush full of vermilion, smash it on the canvas, smearing it in until it picks up the onyx beneath like the heart of a woman.

"I hear your daughters have been in the woods," Roy says.

Shut your goddamn face, are my thoughts. "Really," I say.

"Why didn't they come in?"

"Who would want them sullied by such a gathering of degenerates?"

Roy stays silent for a while but not long enough before he asks where the girls came from.

I ignore him. I don't have to answer anyone's questions. They've come from the bowels of the earth. But then something occurs to me, and I ask him where he will go when we leave the woods.

He shrugs his shoulders and looks over at the door as if he expects someone. "I don't know," he says. "Where are you going to go?"

"I'm going to get my sailboat back on the water. Sail the San Juan Islands and down to Mexico."

"I like the sound of that. I want to ride a horse across the Americas to Tierra del Fuego and sell my art in every town as I go."

"Have you ever even been on a horse?" I ask.

"No," he says. "Why would that matter?"

—

The melodic intertwined cords of my daughters' voices singing *Old Man* tear me out of a dead sleep. I get up and hope the singing is just a strange sticky vestige of a dream that continues to cling in the air of the woke world. Out a knothole in one of the wallboards, there is only dark. Is it now they've come to kill me? Surely this must be their objective, to slit my throat and laugh as I gurgle my last breaths. I won't give them the satisfaction. With two cooking pots in hand, I go out onto the front path and bang them together, to scare the evil spirits away. Moonlight glows off the wet bark of the forest. For a split second, I believe I see the flash of a white robe. With a fiercer determination, I smash the pots.

"You will not get me!" I yell. "You will not get me!"

I smoke cigarettes and pace along the path in front of the hovel. The sound of their singing can still be heard but has grown faint. Is it a trick, I wonder. Are they only singing softer but steadily growing closer and nearer to me? Like the devils they are, closer and closer. I will sink a knife into their eyes and hearts. I will sink my teeth into their flesh. They will not get me.

Thomas comes out of the hovel and asks what the racket is all about.

"My daughters are out there. They have come to kill me," I say.

"Not if Roy gets you first," he retorts.

I ignore his paltry attempt at humour.

"Good luck," he says and tramps off into the woods.

When I turn my attention back to where I thought the voices had come from, the girls are all there. If they are actually my daughters, perhaps they have been possessed by demons? Their white forms ripple amongst the trees like ghouls, with skin frighteningly luminescent. Their lips pressed together, they no longer sing but hum that gawd awful Neil Young tune. A song that has always grated my nerves. I bang the pots and step closer, and they rise up into the trees as if pulled by some invisible cord, like some trick of the theatre. Even my youngest, Cedar, does not come to me. "Cedar," I call.

I'll admit, Cedar is my favourite. Of my three daughters, she and I spent the most time together, and she had the mildest disposition. She is the most of this place—rocks, ocean, dark roots. As was her mother. So much they're alike—thick long hair, high cheekbones, eyes the colour of granite. As a baby, she played on the studio floor while I painted. She was a bundle of inspiration. Her mother knew how to be with an artist. She didn't cry or badger me for things or act out for attention. She knew my energies had to be spent on the canvas, not playing house. As Cedar grew up, she would come visit her father, bringing goods from the bakery or groceries. She always arrived with something to offer. The others never brought gifts, only complaints.

It had occurred to me, when the sailboat was back on the water, that Cedar might want to accompany me on my sail through the islands or to the south. But I guess not now. Not now that she's turned her back to me and joined her sisters in their plot.

THOMAS

Today my wife visits. I call her my wife although we aren't married. There's never been a ceremony. She's all west coast, saltwater, misty fjords, and wolf-like, wild-eyed. Her black hair is laced with grey. She brings poems she's written that tell me of her days: coffee in the morning, dates with friends and writers, and how our daughter suffers. How can my wife still love me? She asks me what I've written, and I provide her with one sad sheet of stained paper. A poem for Iris.

"Why won't Iris come and see me?" I ask.

"She's been trying to see you all her life," my wife says.

What can I say? I know I've failed.

We go for a walk to get out of the shelter and to leave Charles and Roy behind. She's not fond of either of them. Roy has a fractured soul, she says, and Charles is a dog whose nips she cannot stomach. There's a particular rock we like to perch on and take in the ocean with all its blinding light. For some time we sit in silence.

"How long will this stage last?" she asks.

"I don't know," I tell her, but I feel an end is near. "I have no vision for what will come next."

She nods her head and holds my hand. "Will you stay here, or come home?"

Home, I think. I so want to go home. Home, to a bed with clean sheets and my wife by my side. Home, to a healthy and happy daughter. But home exists only in my imagination. It's never there when I arrive. "Home," I say.

My wife is more than I deserve. She's patient and bright. We spend much of our time in silence, and that's fine by me. I was a few months free of the pen when we met in Vancouver, where I'd gone to start over and check out the scene. She was with a group of artists and street performers in Stanley Park on Second Beach. We were instant companions. I knew we would be together until something beyond my control ended our union. If a relationship like ours can't save me from myself, then what hope does man have? And believe me, I've hurt her too. I've caused friends to distance themselves, connections to evaporate, and broken her child.

She's dutifully brought my supply. This she does more out of desperation. I know it, and yet I still let her. I even expect it of her. I know part of her believes I could just quit if I wanted to, walk out of this forest a decent man, go home, and be a father, and a husband. I know this won't happen. It's not possible. Her faith bewilders me.

I asked her to join us at Sombrio, but she wouldn't come. She said she couldn't leave the house where Iris sometimes appears in need of food or money.

We go back to the shelter, and she makes us all dinner—salad with small tomatoes, chickpeas and feta, salmon steaks cooked on the Hibachi. We eat like wild animals. Our diet here at the shelter consists of dried meats, potato chips, and canned drinks.

"Is the world still out there?" Charles asks as if he's on a podium.

"Yes, it's managing quite nicely without you," my beautiful wife says.

After dinner, we smoke a joint and then split a can of peaches. For a moment I can't imagine ever being more content. My wife lights the candles, and I drift off.

—

There's a knock on the door, but when I open it no one is there. I step out into the woods and find Iris, healthy and young, among the trees. I take her into my arms and hold her tight. When I pull back, her face begins to crease and sag, and her teeth blacken with decay. She reaches into her mouth and pulls out a molar. Like it's a glass marble she's found in the garden. She holds it up between us and starts to cry. All the air leaves my body; my chest spasms. I wake in the dark shelter, gasping. The taste of blood in my mouth.

CHARLES

In the early fifties, I found Paris to be full of drunks and blowhards, so I went to Greece. The climate suited me, and the people were less prone to philosophical showmanship. I set up in a small shack that had everything I needed for a studio. I could watch the men launch their skiffs in the morning, and the air was sweet with the scent of lemon-tree blossoms. Sometimes I would take a short stroll up behind the village into the hills and then come back for a Greek coffee at a café. The afternoons and evenings would be spent with my paints. And so the days went by.

On Saturdays, I'd set up at the market and sell small canvases to tourists. Here I could build my skills out of the watchful eye of the world. And here I met the woman who would be the mother of my eldest child, Miranda. Miranda's mother was slim and full of plump in all the right places. I asked her to pose for me, and this was the start of a very creative and happy period. Each afternoon she'd appear, school books still clutched in her arms. I'd paint and consider how it was I could avail myself of her other talents. Eventually there was an affair and then after a few years a child. Miranda was difficult from the start, and her mother grew shrill and tugged at my patience. My thoughts turned back to the Americas.

We left Greece for Canada and struggled to establish ourselves, for several years moving from place to place. There were old friends who had basements or some type of barn where we could live and I would paint. But these arrangements only lasted so long with a wife and child in tow. Miranda's mother found the Canadian climate and economy a tough adjustment from the gentle sun-drenched impoverishment of the Mediterranean. She lacked the social circle she once knew and didn't bother to get out and meet people. Those years saw us in Southern California, Oregon, Washington State, and back to British Columbia. While we were in Astoria, Miranda's mother decided she could find better with a local real estate agent. Reinvigorated and unburdened, I left for an offer in LA to stay in a warehouse that had been re-appropriated by artists.

Once, when I was back in Victoria, Miranda and her mother came to my studio. Miranda must have been around nine years old. She didn't want to step into the room and pushed against her mother's legs in an effort to get away.

"Miranda," I said. "Come say hello to your father."

But she held her mother's legs even tighter. Her mother knelt down beside the child and in an even tone said, "Don't be afraid. He's just your father."

But the sullen girl wouldn't even face me.

"Dad is my father," she said

The girl eventually came over, and we shook hands. There was some resemblance to my mother around the girl's eyes and in the way her shoulders were set. I reached over to my workbench, picked up a piece of rose quartz and handed it to her. "A gift," I said. "For Miranda, my daughter."

She wrapped her hand around the stone and took it out of my palm. "Is this where you live?" she asked and glanced around the studio.

"Yes," I said.

"Why is it so messy?" she said.

And I thought for a moment, the girl had probably been raised in a sterile subdivision, where the houses all look the same. Her mother had a small smirk on her face. "Creative genius does not rise from order, but from disorder and disharmony." I hoped the girl might ask some type of in-depth question about my process, but instead she narrowed her eyes, just like her mother.

"What? That makes no sense," she said. Then she turned to her mother and announced that she wanted to go home.

What a great idea, I thought. Take the bland, washed-out thing away. Bring her back when she's experienced something of the world. Bring her back when we can have a conversation.

ROY

Many things haunt me: an Indian headdress worn by a fat white man, the sensation of sunlight expanding in a room that is too small, the taste of lake water in my mouth. The water, cool and slick on my bruises. As children, we would dive from a dilapidated pier. All of us, sunburnt and flea-bitten, heads shorn with what were called our summer cuts. Somehow, we knew where the rotten pilings were, just under the water's skin. Somehow, we would break up through the surface each time still in one piece.

Remember how we met, Fern? You came up to me, poked my braids, and asked where the pow-wow was. I told you I was going to make you my 'injun' princess. 'Injun' was what my dad called the natives, as if he was a character in some black-and-white western. But you laughed and said, "Don't say shit like that." And I said, I never would again.

"What if I was native?" you said.

"Are you?" I asked.

"1/16 Muktalokatoo."

"Really?"

"No," you laughed. "I just made that up."

We went to my studio, and I showed you my paintings. Then we smoked weed, and I shared with you all the ideas in my head until I realized you had fallen asleep. In the morning, we got coffee and pastries and walked through Ross Bay Cemetery. The air thick with the smell of decomposing horse chestnuts and fallen leaves. We collected shells on the beach and looked out at the strait. We held rocks in our hands and discussed the different types of clouds in the sky. You said the clouds were cirrus, high in the atmosphere. That day is my counterbalance to everything else in my head.

Fern, you've been gone for several days, and I haven't seen you since the party. So, I entertain myself with Thomas. We get high and go drink on the beach. Besides you, Thomas is my best friend. He's the wisest person I know, even though he is an old bank robber. Sometimes he tells me stories of his past exploits. How once they robbed a bank and then drove straight to the airport, bought tickets to Hawaii and stayed in some jungle resort until the heat died down. My favourite stories aren't the ones about the robberies themselves. I don't care about that. I love the stories about what they did with the money. Stories about how they all lived together in a house, girlfriends and all, like a family. How they'd have big barbecues of steak and lobster, and float in their pool at night and gaze up at the stars. These are the stories I like to hear. Stories about things I only saw rich people do on TV.

He tells me one of his 'going straight' stories. How his girl enrolled in a local college and was going to get a degree of some sort. They even had a black lab named Duke. Thomas would come home after robberies and start to make dinner for when his girl came home late from study hall. I can tell these were good days for him because he smiles when he shares the story. I like to see someone smile when they tell a story. So, she's going to school, he's holding up banks, shit is good. Then during a robbery, one of the guys trips down some concrete steps and nearly cracks his head open, and the cops get him. So, the rest of the guys go into emergency mode. They split up and head to Mexico to some agreed-upon nowhere town on the Baja. The girlfriends all know how to clean the house and tie up loose ends, and then they too head for the border.

I don't know why, but somewhere in the midst of this story, my mood really turns, and a thick rage builds in me, real strong, and I just want to kill. Not Thomas, because I love him. But I could just press my hands against his neck, and press and press until his mouth stops and there's no sound. I pick up sticks within arms reach and snap them in half. Break them into smaller and smaller pieces. The pound of the surf is large in my ears, like a moth has flown into my ear canal, and I can't get it out. The flutter of the wings creeps deeper and deeper into my head. I beat the heel of my palm against my ear, but it changes nothing. I beat harder and harder. I want to take a rock and smash it against my skull. I pull down on my braids until there's the sensation the roots will rip out of my scalp, like a large tree blown over in a storm. The roots and earth exposing everything that had previously been a secret to us, embedded rocks, all the dark soil that hasn't seen daylight in centuries, worms, and other critters.

When you do show up, Fern, I want to crush you, hold you so tight that your bones break.

And then Thomas says something, "Hey, I've been thinking about one last bank job."

"Really?" I say.

"Ya, one last job, and then I'd be done with it. And I'm looking for a partner."

I lean closer to him. "I'm in," I say, and then ask what needs to be done.

THOMAS

Dear Iris

I don't know how to be a father. It's taken me till now to be able to put those words together. To be able to realize this is the crux of the problem. I don't know how.

I once spent the day with another writer and his family. He had two children just a bit older than you, but at the time they were six or so. I watched him observe his children kick a ball around. The look on his face, total joy. I asked him what was in his head when he watched his children. He told me overwhelming love and contentment. I asked him if he was ever afraid when they looked him in the eye. No, he said, Never. I wanted to ask him more about how one can learn to feel, 'overwhelming love and contentment' but wasn't sure how to word it. I didn't want to burden him with my problems.

I barely had a father myself. How much this plays into my wretchedness, I don't know, but it can't help. My father was a drinker. What dark shadows followed him I couldn't even say. I knew so little of him. Perhaps there are genetic things I've inherited from him. I don't know. But somehow that only feels like an excuse for my actions. I'm trying to take responsibility. I'm trying to say, everything that happened to you is my fault and my fault alone. And everything that I've done is my fault and my fault alone.

I love you. There's no doubt. But that love is what scares me. My fear of hurting you or not being enough has driven me to hurt you and not be enough. When you were little I would grow anxious when your wide eyes fell on me. They wanted something from me, and I didn't know what it was. So I stayed away longer and longer; the longer I stayed away, the easier it was to do. And then when I came back I couldn't handle your need for me. Did you know small children will look for comfort from the very ones who harm them?

Then the older you got, the hurt rose closer and closer to the surface until it was a layer you wore like a raincoat. I couldn't face your justified rage. But still, you wanted to be with me. Cried for me to stay.

The most offensive crime is, I expected you to be the adult. Expected you to fix me. But I'm the adult and will be so moving forward. I love you, and it's my job to show you that. To love you unconditionally. To hold you when you cry. To say it is going to be okay. To give you hopes and visions of the future. To show you how a man and a father acts. These things I haven't done. But perhaps it's not too late. Perhaps I can make it all up to you.

I've come to the woods to make myself better. And when I come out, it will be to you that I go.

All my love. Forgive me. Actually, don't forgive me. I won't even burden you with such a request. Never forgive or forget a man who has hurt you, like I have.

Deep love
Your Dad
Thomas

CHARLES

Blue, my middle daughter, I barely know. She showed up on my doorstep one day as an adult. Who knows what she expected, but I can say for certain I didn't anticipate her visit. She skulked around for a few weeks. Honestly, I didn't know what to say to the girl. She was like some lost dog. I told her she could hang out in my studio in the mornings with the caveat that I painted and didn't like interruption or distraction. In the afternoon, we would walk down to the café for an espresso. Always, she was agitated, like there was something she wanted to say but wouldn't spit out. Then without warning a question would pop out of her like a sprung spring.

"Do you have any pictures of me?" she asked.

How queer, I thought, Why would she ask such a thing? No, I didn't have any pictures of her. To busy her with something, besides her interrogation of me, I said that any photographs of her would be in the trunk everyone used as a bench. I told her to rifle through and see what she could find.

She opened the trunk's lid and spent two days examining each scrap. There were pictures of me at various stages in life—as an indifferent schoolboy, as a youth on the cusp of striking out to find my own greatness, and on beaches in Europe, California, British Columbia, and Mexico. Every once in a while she held a photograph up and asked who this or that person might be. Usually, it would be some photograph of me as a boy with my parents, sister, and two brothers. She asked where they all were. In the sweet hereafter for my parents and my oldest brother. As for the other two? Who knows. Doing well, I suppose.

"What happened to your brother?" she asked.

"Shot down over Normandy by the Germans," I said.

"During the war?"

Of course, during the war. At what other time have the Germans shot down planes? "Yes, during the war," I said.

She browsed through old ticket stubs for European trains, and for ships that took me across the Atlantic. There were rocks and seashells from places I had forgotten and a copy of *On The Road* signed, *For my pal Charles the artist, Jack Kerouac.* She held the book up and asked if we'd been close.

"We were men," I said.

She placed the book on the carpet, "My mother mentioned you hung out with the beats."

"Sure. I hung out with lots of people," I said and went back to my painting. Had she not heard me when I said I didn't like distraction? She listened as well as her mother did. I could feel her eyes on me, searing a hole through my neck.

"I wish I could paint," she said.

"Then you should," I told her.

"Will you teach me?"

Jesus, her demands infuriated. I pretended not to hear her.

The next day she picked a photograph out of the trunk and asked if it was her.

"No. That is Cedar. She was a glorious infant," I said.

"Oh," she said. "Is she my sister?"

"Of sorts."

"Where is she?" she asked.

"At this moment who knows. She goes where the currents take her."

When Blue got to the bottom of the trunk, and all its contents were spread about in sad stacks, she reversed the process. She studied each item again, every photograph and printed slip, and started to place them all back into the trunk.

"When I die," I said, "light that trunk on fire."

"Why don't we do it now?" she responded.

Ha, I had to laugh. It was the first remotely amusing thing she'd said. Eventually, every little trinket was back in the trunk.

She held up a last photograph and asked, "Who is this?"

"Miranda and her mother in Greece," I said.

"How long ago?" she asked.

"Many lifetimes. You ask too many questions," I said.

She tucked the photo back into the trunk, closed the lid and then perched on top like a crow.

"What are you painting?" she asked.

Goddamn, the constant questions. Would she ask Jesus what his plans were? I dipped my brush into the can of turpentine and then beat the bristles against the leg of an unused easel. "The world," I told her.

And then she was gone, and I have to say it was like the heavy quilt she brought down on me was lifted. I opened all the doors and windows to the studio and left the place to air. I took myself to the beach and spent the day sketching the vast nothingness. Then a strange thing happened that day. When I went back to the studio, Cedar was seated on the floor in the middle of the room. The light shone down on her like she was some fresh sprite from the woods.

"It's freezing in here Dad," she said.

Ah, my Cedar. I held her to me. Her long golden hair, like a chorus of prepubescent choir boys, their voices bouncing about the stone walls of a cathedral. She holds so much light. I asked her if she would stay and paint, and she said she would.

She held up a photograph and asked who was in the picture. I took the photograph from her and studied the image.

"Where did you get it?" I asked.

"Just here on the pillow."

"It's Blue and her mother."

"Who?"

"A child of mine. She was here the last few days, like a flu," I said.

"A sister?"

"Of sorts? She must have left the photograph."

The appearance of Blue was like a poison I couldn't wash off. I could feel the poison in my chest, hard and dark. It burrowed into my organs with its sharp little claws.

ROY

When I was only a month old and my mother a teenager, she took me to a fortune-teller. If my difficulties didn't start with birth, they certainly did that day in the fortune-teller's den. Were it not for that, everything would've been different: my talents would be lauded and I would have great wealth and adoration. Perhaps, my mother would love me.

The fortune-teller looked at the Tarot cards and told my mom that I would cause her nothing but grief and rob her of everything she ever had. And since my mother had nothing of significance, it would be her spirit, hope, and strength that I would take. The fortune-teller even suggested my mother abandon me—leave me in a church or hospital. But my mother couldn't imagine the defenceless infant in her arms could or would cause any harm. Then the fortune-teller said, for one more dollar she would also share the infant's fortune. And so, my mother handed over one more dollar. What the fortune-teller said then I know, because when my mother was in a particularly mean mood or drunk, my fortune would be doled out like punches to the head. How I'd cause much pain to everyone who came across my path, how I'd be haunted by ghosts I couldn't name, how I'd come to an early end, and how I'd be a genius. The genius label, in particular, fired up her wrath. I was called "Fucking genius" so often, I thought it might be my name. Even my siblings called me "fucking genius". It's perhaps the first words I learned to write, scribbled on the inside flap of my elementary school books. Fucking genius.

I went back to this fortune-teller once when I was fifteen or seventeen with a gun. Around the same age my mother was when she sought the fortune-teller's original predictions. My intent was to cauterize this plague that the fortune-teller had let loose with a single bullet to her head. I went up to the house and beat on the door, kicked and punched the cheap wood until my knuckles bled and the door started to splinter. I screamed for the hag to show herself and pelted the house's facade with rocks. Some slob with a grizzly beard leaned out a top window and told me to fuck off or he'd call the cops.

"Where's the fortune-teller?" I yelled.

"Who the fuck knows? Bugger off!" he yelled back.

I picked up more rocks and rained them against the house.

"She ruined my life. I'm going to kill her," I hollered.

And then the cop cars were there, and two officers approached me, each with one hand outstretched like I was a child and the other hand on their guns. They talked in low, smooth voices and asked if I was having a rough night. They said they weren't looking for any trouble. A thought flashed in my mind, to push the barrel of my gun against my own head and let the cool forever night take me. But then I was on my stomach with two cops on my back, arms reefed behind me, dirt in my mouth, bawling my fucking eyes out. When I was in the back seat of the cruiser, they asked what my story was. I had to say I just didn't fucking know, because I didn't. I just wished they'd drive on and on into the night without ever stopping.

THOMAS

I spent ten years on the inside. I know how to live in confined places. Prison is like hell and heaven all mixed together, like a stew that tastes good and then later kills you with botulism. You think you're going to die, but somehow, each morning, breath still enters and exits your lungs.

Prison can almost be a relief, if you close your eyes and don't think about the years you have left. There's a clear list of dos and don'ts with very little grey area. On the outside almost every decision is grey. In prison, it's: get up when the lights go on, eat when you're brought to food, watch when the TV is in front of you, walk when you're outside, sleep when the lights are off. I had lots of time to read, and, due to my somewhat infamous life, most left me alone. I was up there with professional sports figures or celebrities who are or have been imprisoned—Mike Tyson, OJ. Prisoners wouldn't mess with them and didn't mess with me because there had been achievement in our lives. If there's anything that weighs on the mind of an imprisoned man, it's lack of accomplishment.

Prison provides an endless amount of time to consider what you should've been doing with your freedom. People worry about the things that could happen to them in prison like getting stabbed, beaten, or raped. But probably, if you think about it, those things are just as likely to happen on the outside. What people don't consider enough is what won't happen to you on the inside: the ocean swallowing you up, having to provide for yourself or someone else, being hit by a car, being killed by a falling tree, having to look into the eyes of a woman and figure out what it means.

I never had visitors, which was just as well. The men who came back from visitations were burnt-out shells. When you have to sit across the table from your wife, child, or sibling, in a prison visitation room, it's as if all your failures have been dumped there on the table between you. Visitors are a mistake. I got one letter from my girlfriend. She said she'd gone to San Francisco and maybe when I got out I could find her there. I never wrote back. It was too painful. She was a good girl who had run away from a small town. We had running in common. She had long hair and wore ankle-length hippie dresses. Sometimes I think of her and try to imagine what kind of life she might live now. Maybe she's a mom who drives her kids to swim meets and soccer lessons. Or maybe she got on that airplane she always talked about, and went and saw the world. She wanted to be worldly. Maybe she's still in San Francisco. She wouldn't be the girl I left, that's for sure, just as I'm not the boy who left her.

ROY

There I was with all my earnest accomplishments in a portfolio case, marching off to art school where I would learn from the most polished minds. But all I found there were fakes and losers. There was no camaraderie. Everyone was locked inside their little protective shell. I thought we would pool our intellects, discuss the great troubles of the day, and ponder revolution. But instead, everyone was too busy putting purple food colouring in their hair and trying to get a job at the art supply store down the way.

I tried, to the best of my abilities, to put my head down and keep my goals in sight. There were no adoring fans or cheerleaders to spur me on. My mother said art was for idiots and imbeciles. My father was dead and my siblings useless. With nothing more than my own talents, I persevered. I was in the studio early and stayed late. I attended every life drawing night. But as time wore on I began to see the fractures in the system. The spinning wheels of the administration. The damaged egos of the instructors who lived in fear of a student's talent outshining their own. As my work grew in stature, I began to be on the receiving end of more and more abuse and criticism from the faculty. Soon it became obvious that all their petty jealousies would make it impossible for me to remain a student.

There was one particular instructor with a Hemingwayesque appearance who strutted through the studio and picked apart the students' work. He would stand behind me as I worked and say things like, your shadows are not deep enough, think about your intentions, why are you mimicking, and you must find your own form. How could I participate any longer in such a charade?

THOMAS

By car, we're only thirty minutes from the nearest town. I hike out to the main road, and when cars approach I stick out a thumb. But who would pick up a middle-aged man who looks like he's crawled out of the woods? Then a car slows, and a kid leans out the window.

"Need a lift to town?" he says.

They're teenagers and stink of weed. They offer me a puff, and I can't refuse. My mind is left bobbing back and forth in a warm pool of stupid. Trees zip past in a green blur. At times the green breaks to reveal the ocean, and I'm overwhelmed by a nameless nostalgia and could cry if it weren't for the boys in the car.

"What are ya doing?" they ask.

"I'm getting a ring for my soon to be wife," I say.

"Cool man," they chime in unison.

I get out in front of a convenience store and walk a block to the jewelry store. There's a ping sound when I push the door open and step onto the dandelion-yellow carpet. A jolt grabs my gut, and I take a deep breath. Adrenaline wants to course through my limbs. I take note of the two security cameras and then tell myself not to look back at them again. An elderly man with a black suit on, like an undertaker, steps out from a back room and welcomes me.

"Let me know if I can help you with anything," he says.

I can only assume he doesn't recognize me with his calm expression. I buy two simple bands of gold.

Outside, I sit for a bit and smoke a cigarette. Across the street, a man stands on a ladder and attaches a string of Christmas lights to a storefront with a staple gun. My brain is still fuzzy from the weed. I wonder if anyone on the street recognizes me, but so far there's no sign of it. I take out the gold rings and hold them in my palm. They're identical in every way except size.

A gang of kids hang out on the corner. The girls wear tight jeans, and the boys wear black t-shirts without jackets, even though there's a damp chill in the air. One of the girls with long hair has her back to me, and I'm sure it could be Iris. I walk out to the other side of the road and try to get a look at her face. She turns and starts to walk down a side road. I decide to follow her. I would call out to her or yell her name, but my throat won't allow any sound to escape. The girl turns into a laneway behind an apartment complex, and I lose sight of her for a moment. When I step into the laneway, she's there, turned to face me directly.

"What the fuck do you want?" she says. "Why are you following me?"

"I thought you were my daughter," I say and take a few steps back, shocked at her aggression.

"Well, I'm not," she says.

I step further away and say, "Sorry." I want to say more, and tell her how she looks like my daughter, and how my daughter means the world to me, and I have done her more damage than good, but I keep these thoughts to myself.

"Creep," the girl says and spins on her heel and marches away.

If I could just reach out for her and ask her to wait. Ask if she'll let me tell her about my daughter. Maybe she'd have some good advice. Maybe they even know each other. And then I wonder what this mystery girl's father is like. Does she even have one? Perhaps she could come with me, and I would father her too. Iris and this new girl would become part of my clean family when I leave the woods.

ROY

My son was born on an average night, like any other, and his mother gave him an average name—Shane. What point is there in getting mixed up with the naming of infants? Shane, so pedestrian, so unexceptional. The birth was a gruesome affair and continued to be so. More and more, I wanted to be away from the place where those two were locked in some type of shrouded postpartum ritual. Each time I neared the infant, it hollered. I would go to a coffee shop where more stimulating folks gathered. Then I met a fresh face who happened to have a light-filled loft, which I found worked well for my thoughts and paint. Without that child around one could accomplish something.

When the child started to speak and could walk unassisted, I began to take some minor interest in it. On the odd occasion, I'd take him to the coffee shop or a walk on the beach. I'd give him a small scribbler and pencil so he could expand his imagination. Dull little circles and trucks are what he drew. He never became any more dynamic than that.

Later, Shane would show me some poorly executed drawing he'd done of a male figure and tell me about the sad lessons he was getting in art at his school. One of his greatest faults is that he believes he should be praised about every little banal thing he does. I blame his mother for this. She lavished the boy with false praise. A wise move on his part would be to get away from his mother, but there seems to be an unshakable bond.

There was a glimmer in him, around the age of six, where I believed I glimpsed the last true spark of his pure self. Beyond this point, he became polluted by the world. So, I saw him less and less and saw more and more to dislike about him each time.

The last time he came over, he brought a painting he'd done of me. There was something in the thickness of the paint and the crudeness of the lines. I kept that painting up on a shelf for quite a while and studied it. I sat up at night, smoked cigarettes, and gazed at what I couldn't piece together in the work. One night I came home, high on rum, and the sight of the painting startled me. It was as if someone had rampaged through my home, and I knew right there it was evil sent by my son to kill me. I smashed the painting to bits, wood frame splintered across the concrete floor. With a knife, I stabbed the canvas over and over again.

When I woke in the morning surrounded by the violent scattering of debris, I thought, what a waste. I could have painted over Shane's sophomore efforts and put the canvas to better use.

THOMAS

My wife and I go for a walk along the shore. The tide is low and has left quilts of orange and purple starfish exposed to the elements. We find a spot where we're shielded from the wind and sit. Here is where I ask my wife to become my wife officially and give her the ring. Her eyes go wide, and she smiles.

"What?" she says. "Why now?"

I take her hands in mine. "Because I feel things are changing."

She puts the ring on her finger, and I show her the ring I got for myself.

"You left the woods?" she says.

"Yes."

And then I tell her everything about myself, how I was born and my mother thought I was a girl, how my father was a mystery to me and how he died alone. Only after he died did I think to ask him questions about his life. I tell her everything about the shadow and the man who shot himself. I tell her about how I ran away and never looked back and all the broken things inside of me and how I passed these on to our daughter. I assure my wife, I know what must be done now. I will stop the drugs and build my spiritual and physical strength. I promise her that I'll leave the woods a different man. A man she can be proud of. I'll write every day; poems will be the yardstick of my growth. Most importantly, I'll be a real husband and father. The father that Iris deserves and the husband my wife should have. I tell her we must have no secrets.

My wife holds me tight. Her face is so serene and peaceful. Her salt and pepper hair hangs in one thick braid. I ask her to tell me everything about herself, and she does. She tells me how she was born and about her parents. She walks me through her childhood, sailing trips, and dances. She tells me all about lost loves and books she can't live without. She tells me about first sexual encounters, first movies, and her deepest tragedies. All this information I absorb; my love for her only grows. How can I ever know her enough; it's impossible.

When we get back to the shelter, we announce our engagement.

"We must drink to this," Charles says.

We play music and dance all night and only stop when the sun begins to rise and we all find our way to a dark corner to sleep. I hold my wife tight to me and breathe into the soft skin of her neck. I have scattered dreams of being in my childhood home. I'm trying to find something but I'm not sure what. Outside a window, there's the ocean and ships with large sails that anchor offshore. From the ships come men with bows and arrows, and I try to hide. Then I see my daughter. She's in the hallway, and she too has a bow and arrow. She pulls the bowstring back, takes aim at my chest, and then lets go. I gasp for breath and sit straight up. My heart pumps, and I press my hand to my sternum. The shelter is sliced with shafts of light that push through cracks in the boards that make up the walls. Everyone is still asleep. My mouth is dry. I need just one small hit.

ROY

I struggle with reality. I struggle with which memories or thoughts are real. I know it's real when Fern unravels my braids, combs her fingers through the hair to loosen the strands in long soft strokes. Then she re-braids the two ropes so they are tight and true. This I know is real.

We're already high. How this keeps happening I can't even put together. All the steps fall through my fingers and nothing holds in my thoughts when I try to retrace my footfalls. "Did the birds eat your bread crumbs?" Fern would say.

But here we all are, Fern, Charles, and I to witness the joining of Thomas and his wife in some dreamt up union of sky and earth, yin and yang. I couldn't tell you what it's all about or why it needs to happen. Perhaps the impending Armageddon has spurned them on to this nonsense. If none of what we do now will matter in the new world then why bother? Why do any of this? Why get up in the morning? I envision the dirt and rock of the cliffside we stand on giving way, and all of us falling in slow motion to the waves below. I don't believe any of us would scream. We'd allow all our unsaid fears to weigh us down, and each of us would know in our hearts that this was exactly how it should end.

There's no minister, priest, or officiate, just Thomas with his tattered notebook. He starts to go on about cedar boughs that will provide their shelter and how the air will be their blanket. I start to laugh a bit, real quiet at first, little snickers into my palm. Fern kicks my leg. Then Thomas' wife starts to talk about how the moss will be their bed, and then I can't hold back. I let it all out. With my head thrown back, I cackle like a hyena and laugh. The laugh builds and builds until I weep with the comedy. Then Thomas is at me, his fist against my chest. I stumble back, my lungs robbed of air. I go down on my knees, in the dirt. My vision flickers, and I'm certain, out in the forest, there's a shimmer of white. There's a girl out there among the trees, and she too laughs. She looks like Thomas' daughter, and then my sight goes black.

THOMAS

The perfect heist is greater than any high, greater even than any love. When all the plans come together in perfect precision—the arrival is on time, the entrance and threat go off without a hitch, lookouts do their job, the money gets bagged, there is an exit without incident, and no one gets hurt—you can't imagine the exhilaration. If everything goes right, we're gone before there's a hint of sirens in the air. Perfection.

Sometimes small things happen. Maybe there's a stutter or hesitation when wording the demand to the lady behind the counter, or maybe the bank employees freeze and slow the whole thing down, or there's a patron who wants to be a hero. And time is everything. A quick robbery that's sloppy is better than a well-executed robbery that takes twice as long as it should.

I want one last shot. One last take, something small and simple. I get Roy into the idea, tell him how easy it is. How we'll be in and out. How he'll never experience anything else so satisfying. Not sex, not a trip, nothing. We'll split the bag, and then he can do whatever he wants. Now he wants to talk about it all the time. We draw up plans and review our options. Then we revise the plans. We expect to be legendary. Come out from the forest to steal and then fade back into the mountains, never to be seen again. They'll tell stories about us on the playground and at night, around the campfire, just like D. B. Cooper. My calling card left behind, so there's no doubt it was the 5 o'clock gang, resurrected, as if out of thin air. My face back on the TV to disrupt sedate living rooms in the suburbs. I'll be there to remind their dull life what it is to really be alive, alive in a way they will never be.

Through the night we plot and build our scheme. When the elation reaches its peak, we run down to the beach and drench ourselves in the ocean. The thick Pacific rakes my skin, and I scream and scream. Roy screams too, probably he thinks this is some fun form of expression like howling at the moon. But I scream because the sound of the waves as they hit this dark beach is too beautiful. I scream at the pinpoint stars for continuing to exist. I scream because I hate myself and wish for the ocean to rip the skin from my bones. I wish for a sea creature to pull me deep down under the foamy depths and drag me along the seafloor to Japan. Everything for once would be truly dark, complete and absolute darkness—down at the bottom of Marianas Trench, no limbs, no eyes, no weight, just nothingness.

I tackle Roy and hold him down under the water and smash my fist into his skull again and again. He reaches out toward me, his arms flailing, his fingers overextended; he swings blindly. I let him go, and he pops up in a rage with his fists high, his chest puffed out, and choking on saltwater.

"You fucking moron," I yell at him. "Charles slept with your girl."

"No he didn't," he cries, snot on his face. "No, he didn't."

"You're girl's a slut," I say, even though I don't believe it to be true. My wife says 'slut' is an antiquated term.

"Fuck you," he spits out. "Fuck you." He storms up the beach. The sand sucks at his feet, slowing down the momentum of his anger. Soon he's eaten by the dark and the forest.

I'm left with the waves, sand, and rock. Why does anyone like the sound of crashing waves? It sounds like hell beating me over the head.

CHARLES

Thomas sulks in the corner and licks at some unknown wound. On the rug, with a sketch pad, Fern sits cross-legged. Roy is nowhere to be seen. Fern should be on the hunt for her 'partner'. Why is she here when Roy is AWOL? I don't know. Thomas unwinds himself and sits with me in front of my painting. He pours me a drink, which I am happy to imbibe. On a night like this, there's a cozy feel to our hovel. If Fern wasn't here and her female taint, the night might be perfect.

Thomas takes a drink of his vodka and says to me, "Have you ever been in the Michoacán mountains of Mexico and seen the monarch butterflies?"

He knows I haven't, but I can tell he's in the mood to talk. He tells us about hitchhiking through Mexico and how the butterflies covered the trees and he stood inside a cloud of their golden wings.

"That must have been amazing," Fern says and leans in to hear more of the story.

"After that, I ended up in LA, and remember the King Eddy?" he says to me. "That's where we met."

Of course, I remember. I place a hand on one hip and sweep the other through the air. "Yes," I say. "I will never forget that night. I was there with a group of friends, and we were going to drive out to the desert to do peyote. We were all seekers, searching for the greatest adventure. Thomas came in with a sack over his shoulder and long wild hair. I got to talking with him, and he told me how he had just been to Mexico to see the monarchs. The way he described his adventure was mythical. And then, of course, we figured out we were both Canadian— he a prairie boy and me a born-of-the-sea west coaster. And remember, Thomas, I asked you what your trade was, and you said, totally deadpan, bank robber. Jesus, that was a laugh, and I got the bartender to pour us each a shot and said, 'You're coming with us. We're going to the desert to trip on peyote.' And you did not hesitate for a second. You said, 'When we leaving?' And I said, 'Right after this shot.' Now here we are. Giants." I grab the half-full bottle of vodka and top off everyone's mug. I hold my mug high in the air and call out, "To us giants." We knock our mugs together and take deep swigs.

"Old friend," Thomas says. "We just glided through the world then, didn't we?"

"We're still gliding," I say.

"I can't believe you've both known each other for so long," Fern says.

Thomas raises his mug again. "Over thirty years."

"You must know each other very well," she says.

"As well as any man can know another man," I say. "It's not like I know his favourite colour or anything."

"Oh, too bad," Fern pouts and then turns to Thomas. "What's your favourite colour, Thomas?"

Thomas gazes off for a moment as if to give Fern's question some real consideration. "I've always liked green."

"Amazing," I say. "Now I feel so much closer to you."

"How do you guys know you're friends?" Fern says.

"Jesus," I say. "You ask the dullest things." I turn back to my painting and only want silence now, to work. I can only hope they find some other way to entertain themselves other than to vex me.

"Time," Thomas says. "Only time. We knew enough people in the same circles that overlapped, so over the years we would end up in the same spots." Thomas chuckles a bit to himself and then says, "Hey Charles, remember that place in Oregon, and your wife, at the time, lost her mind and smashed the living room window with a chair? We had to call the cops to drag her out of there."

I laugh to think about it. "That was Blue's mother. She was mad because I sold a painting I created for her."

"She was spitting fire," Thomas chuckles.

"Why did you sell her painting?" Fern asks.

I have to close my eyes for a moment. God, her questions. "It wasn't her painting. I painted it for her but not to keep."

"How can you paint something for someone but not let them keep it?" she says.

"It's not that kind of gift. It's more the honour of having a painting created for you by a great artist."

"I'm not sure that's really much of an honour," she says and laughs.

Even Thomas chuckles to himself. I'd like to banish them both from the hovel. They're like monkeys who need constant preening.

"This painting here," I say and point to my canvas, "is for Cedar."

"But she's not going to be able to keep it?" Fern asks. "Does she even know it's for her?"

"No," I say.

"And she's not actually in the painting?" Fern says.

"No."

"OK, why is this supposedly such a great honour?"

Thomas watches this exchange with rapt attention.

"In the future, when this painting is in an important gallery or replicated in books, I'm sure Cedar will be mentioned in the byline in association with the painting."

"And that's an honour?" Fern prattles.

But here I've had enough of this whole conversation. Why I've even entertained her at all, up to this point, is beyond me. She holds no more interest to me than paste. It's enough to hope for Roy's return to divert her focus.

Then she pipes up again. "Why are you and Roy friends?" she says.

"We aren't," I say. "He's my apprentice."

"You can't be friends too?"

"I suppose we could, but I don't very much like him."

"He thinks you're friends," she says.

"He can think what he wants, but I wouldn't call us friends."

"That's funny," she says. "He really believes you're deeply connected."

THOMAS

Inside the shelter, near my dark corner where I like to perch, I start to dig a tunnel into the earth. I can see no other place to go but down. With a rusty spoon, I scrape away at the black earth, deeper and deeper. I hack through roots and remove large stones until there's a chamber that I can hide in. The thick root of a mighty hemlock acts as my chair. I light the space with candles and line the floor with newsprint. It's a fine spot that I've managed to keep a secret from the others. Even my wife is unaware.

Everyone needs a place that's all their own, a place no one else can see. I keep my most precious books here: *Junkie, Big Sur, Tropic of Cancer, A Season in Hell*, the plays of Sophocles, *Waiting for the Barbarians*. They sit on a small shelf carved into the earth. The pages within are thin and worn, specific words and sentences underlined, notes in the margin, the corners bent. Every once in a while, I'll take a book and open it at random and pray that what I might read there will reform me or provide me a guide as to how to be in this world.

Fern arrives with more dried meat and canned soup. I like to believe that only Fern and my wife can see the trail that joins road and shelter. I like to believe that there's no way out of the forest for me. That if I tried to leave, the trees would come together to block my path. I'd wander the woods, disoriented, the undergrowth pulling me back until, lost, I travelled in a wide circle, and arrived back at the shelter. All life in the forest wants me to stay.

Days stretch out and then weeks. It's unknown to me how long I've been here. In the woods, there's a magic that suspends time, like prison. No one ages in our shelter. We're all our best day, our best self. I am six and then twenty-seven. I am tanned skin, barrel chest, clean lungs. I'm an infant fresh from my mother's womb and at rest in her arms. Although, my mom always said they knocked her out for my birth. When they brought me to her several days later, she didn't believe I was the infant she birthed. She was certain she'd delivered a girl. She told the nurse that the doctor had shown her a girl. The nurse said this was impossible. She'd been unconscious. My mother agreed but said she never shook the thought that out there somewhere was her baby girl and I was not her child. Mom held me out under the fluorescent lights and could see I was perfect. My chest moved with my heart, and my fingers reached out to grab whatever they could.

In my cave, I imagine how the world will be after the collapse. In my heart, I imagine that none of the doomsday scenarios will happen but I will be different. I will be clean, and Iris will come home, and we'll be a family.

ROY

I never trusted that good for nothing, talentless snake, piece of shit, low life. When I find him, out in the woods, I push him and call him a scumbag. He acts indignant as if he has no idea what this scuffle is about.

"Keep your hands off Fern," I tell him.

He laughs long and hard, like I've told a good joke and slaps his thigh.

"This isn't a fucking joke," I say.

"Sure it is," Charles says. "How would Fern be able to resist my charms? You should talk to your gal. She has got a mind of her own. She's independent, so they say."

"I'm talking to you dip-shit. You go near her again and I'll knock your head clear off."

"Perhaps she pursued me," he says.

"She wouldn't do that, old man," I say.

"Really," he says. "She wouldn't? Fern has told me all sorts of things about you."

"She hasn't."

"She has. All your sad little thoughts."

I know Fern wouldn't do this. She's too good. Too good to conspire with this garbage. I want to strangle him, to push him down onto the moss-covered ground and press my heel against his old brittle chest until I feel it crack under my weight. Who would miss him? Not us here. Not anyone on the outside. He has no one. His daughters don't talk to him. They stopped years ago, along with their mothers. He has no one.

"She has quite the pert set," Charles says.

I lunge forward, my limbs possessed by a violent desire out of my control. My hands wrap around his neck and squeeze and squeeze. He's under me, and I can feel the force in my hands. The look on his face is more amusement than fear. I want to crush the amusement right out of him. I pull a handful of hair from his head and then back away from him. I spit on him and tell him that if he goes near Fern again I'll kill him.

"You will only feed my legend," he says. "Death was a boon for Van Gogh."

"You're no Van Gogh," I say. "You're not even the men who hung their paintings beside Van Gogh's and have now been forgotten. You're less than all of them."

He dismisses me with a flick of his hand like I'm some disobedient child. I spit at him again and walk away, a clutch of his long yellowed grey hair in my fist.

When I see Fern I'll get the truth, because she can't be dishonest with me. Everything that comes out of Charles' mouth is a lie. What could he possibly know about Fern? She would never divulge anything to him. Although I have no doubt that he'd try to seduce her. Charles can't function without the spotlight of a woman's gaze upon him. That's why I admire Thomas. He's a man of solitude and only desires the love of his wife. He's a junkie to be sure, but also a monogamist. This must be mostly due to who his wife is. She comes into the woods only when Thomas needs to be restocked. Curious that she's his trafficker. Always, they slink off to someplace in the forest together. Their conversations and thoughts are known to no one but them. She must have some type of spell over him. He's like a puppy dog on a leash when she's around. I wonder what they talk about? I should study her more closely. After all, it must take a very special woman to turn a man away from all other temptation. Although I adore Fern, she does not hold all my confidences. How could she? She's a flower, and I'm a mountain.

THOMAS

There are days I walk for as long and as far as I can along the shore. I climb over rock outcrops, jump across crevasses and wade through tidal pools. I live off the land—huckleberries, salal and salmon berries—and drink water from errant streams. Sometimes I stop and try to sort out my thoughts. If you thought back over your life, what do you think would've been your very first mistake? Robbing that first bank, stealing that first car, running away from home, accepting a ride from a shadow?

But what was the true mistake? That I wanted more of life? Was it that I left the house that morning or was it that I got out of bed? Was it a few days before, when the shadow bought popsicles for the boys in front of the hardware store? I took the popsicle, was that the mistake? The heat that day was intense, and the popsicle melted sticky orange-coloured liquid down my arm. Then we ran off into a field and split up into Nazis and Allies. Kill the Krauts. The afternoon spent covered in dust and sweat, over and over we killed each other with the sticks we pretended were guns.

Ahead on the trail comes a jangle sound like some kind of carnival. Soon the ruckus makers come into sight, two hikers with bear bells wrapped around their ankles. They stop dead in their tracks when they spot me. I'm sure they wonder if I'm real or not and try to calculate the level of threat I carry. I continue toward them, and they too begin to walk, although slower now.

"Hi," one of them says.

They're resplendent in the latest hiking attire. Myself, I'm in old jeans and a t-shirt, shaggy hair, and beard, with no backpack. I pass by them without a word. What could we possibly exchange, small talk about the weather? I am sure our crossing is enough to provide one wild story for them, the crazy man they ran into on their hike.

When I'm exhausted, I collapse on a bed of mossy earth and sleep and sleep and sleep. Eventually, I'm woken by damp and cold. I sit up and shake my body. Thankful for the hours of darkness in my head. Across the way, in the gloom of the forest, there's a wolf with white fur. The wolf watches me as I watch it back. Then it saunters away and leaves me with no answers.

I start to head back and climb again over the same rocks and jump over the same streams.

Hours pass by, and I spot Charles ahead on the trail. He has a palm pressed against his shoulder.

"That ungrateful shit," he says.

"Roy?" I say.

"Who the hell else. I hope he falls off a cliff."

"You slept with Fern," I remind him.

"Who cares," he says. "There is no Roy and Fern. They are just two people. Nothing else." He passes me and continues on the trail, then yells back that I should watch my back around the hovel and that Roy is a fucker.

I cut up through the forest and into the deep coolness. There's an area that opens up under the canopy, and I sit on a fallen tree. Then I spot Fern. She steps into the clearing from a trail on the northeast side with a pack on her back full of supplies. She would walk right past me if I didn't call out to her. She stops and scans the surroundings and then sees me.

"Thomas," she calls. "What are you doing out here?"

"Just sitting," I tell her.

"All right," she says and comes over and sits on the log beside me.

"You may have some trouble between Roy and Charles," I say.

"Oh," she says but doesn't add anything more. We sit for a while and inhale the rich air.

"How's your daughter?" she asks.

"Suffering," I say. It's the only answer.

"Is she getting better?"

"I don't think so."

"I'm sorry to hear that. I see her every once in a while in town."

"Do you know her?" I ask.

"No, not really. We have some people in common," she says.

"Bad people?"

"Just people," she says.

We sit in silence, and I reconsider my walk and wonder if I should have walked for longer. I ponder what it was in me that caused me to turn back. Why? What is it that draws us back to whatever place we're calling home for that moment.

Fern leans back and for a second kicks her feet off the ground. "Do you ever wonder, when you're sitting somewhere, what might have happened in this very spot like a thousand years ago?"

I blink and wait for the words she has said to make sense in my brain. "No," I say.

"I do," she says. "All the time. Like this spot here in the woods. Maybe once, a long time ago, this was a meadow, and two lovers came here, but they had a fight and the ground was stained with their tears. Maybe the very tree we sit on was just beginning to form and absorbed their pain, and now we're feeling their trauma but just don't know it."

I sit with what she's said, and somewhere in my chest I feel she might be right. We're haunted by everything that has ever happened in this world: wars, acts of God, economic collapse, famine, and plague. We're all the outcomes of chance, disaster, and misfortune. "I lived in an apartment that was haunted," I tell her. "I always had the exact same nightmare the entire time I lived there. It was awful. I would dream I was being covered with dirt, like being buried alive. The lights would turn on by themselves, and there would be noises that came from in between the walls. I knew something bad had happened on that land once. I sensed it wasn't from the apartment itself, but the very soil the place was built on."

"Ya, you get it. I think our bodies are the same. I carry everything from my ancestors—witch burnings, genocide, slavery. It's all there beating in my heart."

"What hope do we have?" I say.

She shakes her head. "I don't know."

We watch the light filter down through the canopy and crawl across the forest floor, and we listen to the chatter of forest life. Fern stands up and says she has to go. She hikes the strap of her backpack higher onto her shoulder, takes a step backwards and says she'll see me later at the hideout.

I nod my head, distracted with the deep need for a hit that has begun to crawl across my skin.

She turns back to me, "I forgot, I have this friend, Shane, who wants to meet you. He's a big fan, and I told him I know you. Is it alright if I bring him by?"

"Big fan of what?" But I know what it will be.

"You know, the bank robbing."

"Of course," I say. What else is there to be a fan of.

ROY

Everyone here has lost their minds. Charles, I'll kill when I get a chance, and Thomas has dug himself a hole in the earth. For myself, I've decided I will go up, into the sky. There's a tree, not far from the shack, that's taller than all the others in the area. On the trunk, I nail the clump of hair ripped from Charles' head, like a talisman. Then I start to nail pieces of board, one-by-one up the trunk to fashion a ladder. Each board takes me a foot higher. It's slow and rough work, but eventually I'm high in the canopy. Among the top boughs, I build a wood box with about four square feet of floor space. The top can be opened and closed to protect against the elements.

With stealth, I slip back into the shack and take the items that are precious to me—a rock from a place whose name will not come to me, two eagle feathers, and an abalone shell with a bundle of sage. I climb back up into my watchtower and sit cross-legged on the floor. With my hands at rest on my knees, I take a few deep breaths into my lungs. Then I light the sage. The smoke wafts over my bare chest and face, and I inhale its sacred scent. I wave the smouldering sage bundle in every corner, purifying my new home.

Finally, I collapse onto the floor and sleep, exhausted by my efforts. During the night I have a dream where I'm making love to Fern and in the midst of our intimacies, she turns into the mother of my son. Later, in the same dream, I'm running on a gravel road through some town and then a city I can't recognize. The crash of waves and the squawk of eagles wake me, and it's as if I have woken in the heavens, one of the chosen in the new world. For as far as I can see the ocean rolls out like a paradise earth.

THOMAS

After a robbery in Ventura, we went to a drive-in for food. We had the appearance of a car full of college kids, out for some burgers and milkshakes. The Beach Boys played on the radio, "Good Vibrations". I went inside the restaurant to use the bathroom, and on my way back to the exit a kid caught my attention. He was seven or so with cut-off jeans for shorts, his blonde hair in a crew cut. I stopped and sat in one of the booths to watch that boy. For a split second, our eyes met, and I saw all I needed to know. At once, I knew we were the same, that everything he was living and experiencing was everything I had already known.

A man with a yellow t-shirt on and dirty jeans tapped the boy on the shoulder, and they went out to where the cars were parked. There was a hot flash behind my eyes, and it was as if a crack broke through my entire body. I followed them out into the heat and came up behind that man and smashed his head with my fists. He buckled to the pavement, and I kicked him over and over. The only thing that stopped me were my guys who pulled me away and forced me into the car. I forget who was at the wheel, but they drove out of there so fast, the force pushed me back against the seat. No one spoke until we got home and we were all out of the car, standing on the driveway.

"What the fuck?" one of the guys said. "What the fuck, Tom?"

But I didn't know what to tell them. I hung my head and told them to get over it. How could I explain to them how I knew the boy was being molested by that man? That the same thing had happened to me, once upon a time. Inside the house, I drank all the booze I could find. For days, I was like a wild animal on a rampage. The guns called out to me. We kept them down in the basement under a wood counter, and I could envision them there, in the dark, wrapped in burlap. Over and over they called my name and asked me to come and get them. Visions repeated in my mind, the metal trigger against the curl of my index finger, and the barrel against my temple.

When I was a boy, back in my hometown, there was a man who blew his brains out. People in town said he had stormed the beaches of Normandy and done many other heroic things. I couldn't understand it. Why would a hero kill himself? Why would a man who had survived enemy fire shoot himself? A bunch of us clambered near the house and tried to get a look through the bedroom window, where it was rumoured the wall was covered with blood and brains. The cops shooed us away, so we ran off into the scrub and boasted to each other, how we would never be so stupid as to kill ourselves, especially if we were a hero. Heroes, if they were smart, got all the girls and became movie stars like Rock Hudson.

Every time I walked by that house, on the way to school, I thought about that man and wondered why he did it, and wondered if I could do it too. Could I pull the trigger? Over time the images and thoughts morphed in my brain until I became the man with the gun to his head. Over the years, I have lost count of how many times I've put the barrel to my head. But that time in Ventura, after the boy, that was the first time. The first time I picked a gun up with the intent of using it on myself. I sat there on the basement floor, with a bottle of whiskey and the weight of the gun in my hands. I cried and wanted everything to be black, all the mixed-up thoughts and emotions to stop. I wanted an answer for all the world's unanswerable questions.

ROY

From my watchtower, I spy Garth, Charles' gallery agent on the trail heading toward the shack. I throw a pinecone at him and hit him on the shoulder. He stops and gazes up into the treetops.

"Garth," I holler. "Charles is a talentless, backstabber."

"I was looking for you," he yells back.

"Why?"

"Last time I was here, I saw some of your work and thought it would fit an upcoming exhibit."

"I'll be right there," I say and scramble down the rungs of the tree, dropping onto the forest floor.

We decide to go over to the shack and review my paintings. Inside the shack, I gather my canvases, take them outside, and lean each one against the pyramid of firewood.

Garth paces back and forth and studies them at different angles, then stops in front of a painting of abstract geometric shapes and braces his chin like he is Rodin's, *The Thinker*. "Tell me about your education?"

"Emily Carr, but I never finished."

He shrugs his shoulders. "Some of the best artists never finished art school."

"There were irreconcilable differences between myself and the establishment," I add.

We talk for a while about Jasper Johns, who also never finished art school. Flags and numbers, I call him, old flags and numbers.

Garth pulls out a notebook and jots something down. "What are your plans?"

"To paint, nothing more, nothing less."

He nods his head. "I'll take everything," he says. "When do you think you'll all come out of the woods?"

"There's no set date. We'll see what's left of the world in the new year."

"I'm sure it will be just as it is today," Garth says.

"But how do we know? Every religion in the world says one day Armageddon will reign and only a select few will rise to start the world over."

"I'm not sure that's true, that every religion has a doomsday scenario."

What does Garth know? Who is he anyway but a man who lives off the talents of others because he possesses none of his own? He's a leech. Finally, he takes the paintings and starts to head back to the road. I watch him until he disappears amongst the trees. Next time he comes our way, I hope it's only to give me a pile of cash; otherwise, I don't want to see him again.

CHARLES

Thomas keeps going on about a storm predicted for New Year's Eve. Perhaps he speaks metaphorically out of some drug-fuelled delusion? I don't know. What disturbs me most is not the thought of a storm. After all, this coast has weathered many a storm. What unsettles my soul is a dream I had last night, where three dogs tore at my flesh. When I woke, my blankets, at the end of my cot, were soaked with rain water that had dripped through the roof. I got up from bed and painted the heads of snarling dogs on the three figures. For the rest of the morning, I painted until the rain ebbed off and sunlight broke through the gaps between the wallboards.

What was strange about the dream was that I sensed my sister's presence. She didn't make herself seen. She was only an eerie pull in some place at the back of my brain. I decide to walk into town to clear away the dream's latent residue. Town is drab and even drabber with its pathetic smattering of yule, sad lights slung around doorways, plastic holly branches in store window displays. At the single derelict pay phone I dial the operator to make a collect call to my sister, Noreen. A young voice answers, and for a moment I think it's one of my own daughters. The operator clicks in and asks if she'll accept a collect call from Charles.

There's silence on the other end, and then the girl calls out to someone else, "It's a collect call, Nan. I don't know who it is."

Then there are shuffle sounds and a new voice says, hello, Noreen's voice. Again, the operator says there's a collect call from Charles. And again silence, and then Noreen says, "Okay, I'll accept." At the edge, Noreen's voice sounds so much like mother, our mother.

"Noreen," I say.

"Who is this?"

"Charles."

"Charles, who?" she asks

"Charles, your brother."

There's a good long silence, and unsure what to do, I decide to tell her how I'm on the coast working on what is to be my career-defining piece of art. I even tell her I'm there with a few friends, another painter, and a poet.

"That's nice," Noreen says. "You have to excuse my shock. It's been over twenty years since I heard from you. You didn't even come to mom's funeral."

A heat rises in my chest at the mention of the funeral. I was at an artist colony in Argentina at the time. I feel like she's trying to push my buttons. "I called to ask about Father," I say.

"What about him?"

"Did you know he wasn't our real father?"

"Charles, really? This again? He was our father, the only father we had."

"Genetically, I'm saying."

"I know what you're saying. I don't know what you're after. Do you wish he wasn't our father? Would that make you feel better?"

"But Uncle Peter said he wasn't," I say and hear something in my voice that makes bile rise up in my throat.

"Maybe he did. Who cares? What difference does it make? Our parents are dead," she says.

"The difference would be that I would know who my actual father was, or at least I could attempt to find out."

"Charles, is this the only reason you called? And collect at that?"

"Didn't you find Father distant? He didn't often talk to me."

"Fathers were distant then. I don't know. I don't feel like I knew him myself."

"Once I crashed my bike into a tree, and I went to him and tried to hug him, and he backed away from me."

"Charles," Noreen hisses into the receiver. "Enough of this. Put it to bed. He was there day in and day out. We had a roof over our head, clothes, and food. We went to private schools, Charles. My kids didn't go to private schools. Did yours?"

I feel as if she's yelling at me now for no reason. "I was just trying to have a conversation with you, Noreen," I say. "But I see this is not possible."

"Consider your daughters, Charles. They've been to visit and they're broken. Consider the havoc you've raised them with. Did father ever do that to us? No. You need to worry yourself more about the trouble you yourself have caused. Consider the messes you've created."

"You know nothing about my daughters. And I would prefer you didn't meddle."

"Meddle? They come to me when they can't find you," she says.

Now I've had enough and tell her I'll call her another time when she's not so riled up and hang up the phone.

The sight of the damp store fronts insults me. I go over to the diner for a cup of what they consider coffee in this town.

—

As a child, my father was the man in a room with a closed door. On the odd occasion when the door was open, I'd peek into the room, knowing better then to step over the threshold. He would be at his oak desk, absorbed in what I could only imagine were mysterious things, adult things. The drapes would block out all the light, and he would have one small desk lamp on. He never acknowledged I was there. So what that he paid for private school? I'm sure he'd have been at a loss to say where the school even was. What kind of life was that? Every day in that dark house with its wood-panelled walls and ornate furniture no one was allowed to sit on. My daughters, on the other hand, were born in the wild open world, with sticks in their hair and dirt on the bottoms of their feet. Their education, I'm sure, was better than any lesson I studied at school, with its ties and scratchy wool trousers. Those girls are the earth, and they have no gratefulness for it. Why would they visit Noreen? She can't do anything for them. Noreen shouldn't allow it. She should send those girls on their way. Honestly, they'll stop at nothing. Perhaps, I should do as my own father did, find a room and close the door to them.

—

When I broke free from my parents, I sailed across the Atlantic, in homage, to visit the continent that had taken my brother away from me. I showed up on the front walk of my father's brother's home in Norwich, northeast of London.

The house was quite grand, and I gave the large wood door three sharp knocks. The man who answered, my Uncle Peter, was a mirror image of my father. He was warm and jovial and pulled me in for some supper, served by my aunt Grace. We discussed tidbits, what I had scheduled to do while in Europe and my plan to pursue art. He told me he had worked for the city in the land tax department. After supper, we went for a walk into the countryside that stretched out behind his property. He said he had something to show me, up over the way. We trudged up a steep rise, and on the other side was the enormous broken and twisted body of a B-24 Liberator.

"Ten men lost," my uncle said and shook his head.

We went down to the wreck and circled the site. The tail portion had broken apart from the rest of the body and sat some way off. The nose was plowed into the earth, the propellers, twisted and mangled. I took a step into the fuselage and touched the metal supports and thought of my brother. He must have seen such planes, maybe even been inside them.

"These were combing the coast for u-boats," Peter said and then continued on about the bombs that fell on Norwich.

But I was lost in thought, for what reason was my brother really over here? Did he have grand intentions, pure ideals? My brother would be held up as a hero regardless of who he may truly have been. I couldn't ever have really known him. What can a child know about the interior motivations of anyone? I turned to gaze out over the green hills and blue sky and knew that I would have to obtain a greatness that couldn't be debated. No one debated Renoir's greatness. His was a greatness without question, a greatness that eradicated everything that lay around it. Did anyone know or care if

Renoir had siblings? Then a firm hand came down on my shoulder, and I jumped.

"Your brother," Peter said. "This was inconsiderate of me to bring you to a crash site."

"Not at all," I said. "It is very interesting."

We started the walk back to the house, and just for fun, I asked him if he knew if Renoir had any siblings.

"Renoir?" he said. "No idea."

Back at the house, we sat in a regal sitting room, and he spoke of a photograph he'd received from my father when he wed my mother. He began to describe the photograph, how I was in it as an infant, and my sister as a toddler, and my brother. I asked him to clarify, how could my brother, sister, and I have been in my parents' wedding portrait.

He took a big puff of his cigar. "You do know, Laurel is not your natural father?" he said.

Somewhere out in the village church bells began to chime. Cigar smoke hung in the air in wispy layers that undulated up to the yellowed panels of the ceiling. As the church bells subsided, the tick-tick of the Gothic grandfather clock grew and grew in my ears. And the small details of shabbiness suddenly become apparent—the worn damask on the walls, the threadbare carpets, the stained sofa seats, chipped spindle work and the like. Even the very clothes the man wore were ready for the thrift bin. Suddenly I realized how foolish it was to show up on these people's doorstep. I wasn't the son of the man I believed to be my father. I was, as it turned out, completely unaware even of my own biology. I stood up, thanked them for their kindness, and said I had to go. Peter dropped cigar ash across his trousers and jumped up.

"I fear I've given you a shock," he said.

"Not at all," I responded and acted as if this wasn't news that would shake me.

THOMAS

When I look back at my life, it's always the same vision: the dust stirred and lifted from a gravel road, dried out by a prairie sun, tall grass, the smell of hot leather, and the struggle to pull enough air into my lungs, panic that I may never breathe again. The shadow cast by the man in the car has darkened my entire life. Then I'm on that gravel road, and I start to run. My seven-year-old heart pumps blood thinned with warm beer. I just fucking run and run and run. Nothing ever gets closer, not my mother, or my father, or the house where we live. It's just one dry hot dusty road that never ends. And then that same road leads out of town to other places, and to people I tear through.

There's an unbelievable feeling one gets after robbing a bank. It's euphoric. It's your best day multiplied by a thousand. It's your best high. That's why I believe no one ever robs just one bank in their lifetime; you have to repeat the experience. Twelve hours of pure nirvana can be yours; all you need is a gun, a gang, a bank, and a plan.

The first bank I robbed was so easy I couldn't not do it again. It was 1968, and I was nineteen. After the robbery, we hid in the hills inland from San Francisco and waited. Not a thing happened, no sirens, no takedown, no cops. We combed the newspaper, and there was only a small mention. How was it that more people weren't holding up banks? We got maps and came up with guidelines: rob banks in small towns, towns with multiple roads out; never rob more than one bank in a single county. We worked our way up and down the coast: California, Idaho, Oregon, Washington State.

The newspapers started to call us the 5'o'clock gang on account of the robberies going down just before the banks closed for the day. That suited us just fine. We thought it was a real hoot. And then there we were, with money, time, and girls. Like normals, we'd leave the house as if heading into the city for a 9 to 5 and come home with milk, bread, and bags of cash. We grilled steaks by the pool and floated in the water until the stars came out. My girl floating by my side. Both of us dumb enough to think that our lives would always be this way.

CHARLES

It's Fern who comes in and hands me the envelope that she says was pinned to the front door. On the face of the envelope's thin paper is written, "Dad, from Miranda, Blue, and Cedar". I tear at the sealed flap and pull out a letter which I read in silence.

Dear Dad

We've tried to reach you, each in our own way. We've tried to express the things that trouble our souls. We've loved you and found that love squandered. We've tried to be close to you only to be pushed away. We've even tried to leave you behind, but your shadow is dark and heavy on our hearts. So, Father, we have a proposition.

On New Year's Eve, you will burn your masterpiece, and for one year's time you will live alone with Miranda at Sombrio. You will not paint or draw, you will not speak of art. For one year, Miranda will be your only concern. When a year has passed, Miranda will leave, and Blue will arrive. Again you will live together for a year, no art. For the third year, you will be joined by Cedar. This is what we ask of you—three years of your life, one year each, of your undivided attention.

If you reject this proposal then we will disappear from your life entirely. This is your choice.

Forever and always,
Your daughters

What madness is this? Instead of their sly attempts to destroy my career, they've now come out and made a targeted hit.

"What is it?" Fern asks.

I hear her voice like something that has wafted up out of a sewer grate. Unable to vocalize the words needed to outline the plot my daughters have cooked up, I hand the letter to her. I watch her scan the page and try to assess her facial expressions. When she's finished she looks up at me with a smile.

"Brilliant," she says.

"It's blackmail," I say.

"No. They want you, your time, your love. They want to know you. They want a father," Fern says.

"A father? I am their father. We know this. What they want is my soul. They want to eat me alive and crush my bones."

"It's only three years. Take it. Get to know your daughters."

"They won't be satisfied with it. They will still want more."

"Maybe, but they said they'll accept the outcome, no matter what it is."

"It's a trap," I say, and I'm sure of it. Nothing could ever be enough for those girls, never enough time or attention. "I never pestered my father in this way," I say to Fern and then wonder why I'm saying anything to her at all. How has Fern turned into my confidante? Now I know the forest is driving me mad.

"This isn't you and your father; it's your daughters and their father," she says.

"You're talking riddles," I say and hold the letter against one of the log supports, stabbing it into place with a broken fountain pen. I turn to my masterpiece, so close now to perfection, and run a hand over its stippled surface.

"Just burn it," Fern says.

"I might as well pour the gasoline on myself."

"It's nothing but wood, canvas, and paint. In fact, very flammable. Almost as if it were designed to burn."

"Isn't there someone else you can bother?" I say to her.

ROY

I slip down into Thomas' cave and help myself to his stash. A few hours later I'm so ruined I'm not sure if my body is ascending or descending, laughing or crying. My sides expand indefinitely, out, out, like a mushroom cloud. My heart races like a motor. I must get to the watchtower before I lose my ability to keep my thoughts in check. When I surface into the shack, I'm surprised to find Fern. I grab her hand and tell her to bring her stuff because we're going to my watchtower.

"What watchtower?" she says.

We sprint through the woods, Fern just behind me, until we get to the tree. We climb and climb until I am safe inside my box. Fern pulls herself up onto the wood floor then stands and takes in the view.

"This is fantastic," she says.

I take her hand, pull her to me, and hold her close. Pressing my face into her neck, I take in her caramel and turpentine scent.

"What were you doing with Charles?" I demand.

"Charles," she says. "What do you mean?"

"You know what I mean. Did you sleep with him?"

"Gross, that old dog. You got to be kidding me."

And there, now I know Charles and Thomas are liars. Of course, Fern wouldn't allow herself to be defiled by that bag of gas.

—

Fern likes to tell me that I am not special. This is probably why I love her the most. Actually, love is not the right word; love is too soft. I need her. She is like a drug I can't kick. I want to be a part of her, for us to be molded into one form. She's no bullshit. Her body is like a gold-dusted fawn. She braids her long hair into ropes and pins them up in loops on her head. I want nothing

79

more than to pull the pins out, to let the hair fall back into its full wildness. She is lady and beast. She is demure and wild. She is heaven and hell.

"Tell no one about the watchtower," I say. "We must keep it a secret from the great crowd."

"Sure," she says and then pulls from her pocket a block of hash.

We go back to the shack, where there's food. We roll hash and some of Thomas' cocaine into a joint. Soon I feel the fire inside me burn and spark, bright and hot. Fern's limbs grow long, her eyes dark. Her hair becomes a noose to drag me through the forest. Her tongue, hidden in her mouth, has split like a serpent's. Her plump lips call to me. Her soft fingers lure me into her trap. I know that tongue wants to stab itself down my throat, worm its way into my lungs, pull out my larynx, snapping tissue, and vessels. She'll leave me to gurgle blood, and drown, with pink foam on my face, while she pulls my viscera, like a treasure, into her mouth and smacks her lips. Pulls everything into her acid-filled gut in one swallow, like a crocodile. Her black eyes observe me with a cool distance. I grab for my throat, already dead, although my brain is just on the cusp of understanding this. You're not special, she will say.

Then I see something more terrifying than the demon Fern has morphed into; I see my mother. This I can't take. Rage rises in me, stealing command of my limbs. My mother did not love me. She taught me none of the things a mother should. I asked Fern, one night, what she thought mothers were supposed to teach their sons.

She looked at me very seriously. She always takes my questions seriously, and said, "How not to be an asshole."

"But how do they do that?" I asked.

"I don't know," she said. "I'm not a mother, but I imagine with love, decency, respect, and time."

I rolled those words through my mind like a mantra: love, decency, respect, and time. And I wished deeply that my son had been born to Fern and not the other woman. Fern would produce a better result.

I feel the fire and fear in me rise, and my mother grows larger and larger, overshadowing the whole room. She soaks into every surface, every object tainted with her odour. I swing my way through the heat, through the pull at my gut. My fists are heavy and wild, and then I'm under the lake's surface. My nose floods with the taste of a million years worth of decay, and then I'm in my mother's kitchen. Her blows rain down on me. I am a child, so small and frail—just a child. I reach out and grab a knife. For once, I will take this knife and plunge it into the soft tissue of my mother's throat. For once, I will put an end to this weight that always pushes me down. I lift the knife and start to bring the blade down, my sights set on the pale spot at the back of my mother's neck. Then Thomas is in front of me, his hand on my wrist. Fern is on her feet, her eyes large, the skin of her cheekbones red as if she's been slapped.

"Go," Thomas tells her.

She spins around and runs for the door, and then my dear Fern is gone. Tears rush into my eyes, roll down my cheeks, and wet my lips. They taste dirty and ancient in my mouth. I hear myself shout words that even I don't understand, and then I remember to lie still. Lie still so as to not be seen, so as to not be noticed, like a field mouse. Like a small boy in the kitchen with the weight of a cookie sheet smashing down onto his head. Lay still. Perhaps your father will come after all, as he promised, and take you to his new place, where he lives with the girlfriend you've never met. She'll cook warm meals and read bedtime stories and no longer allow you to go to the lake. Because the lake is dangerous, as are so many other things out there in the world, for a little boy.

THOMAS

At the cliffs I smoke a laced joint, and the night air begins to pulse and wave. The white fingers of the cocaine hold my heart and caress my lower spine. I am love, I am air, I am ocean, I am moss. This hard earth beat soft. The night is so alive. Insects chirp and buzz. Birds rustle in the treetops. Whales, not too far offshore, leap into the air. The great rounds of their backs and knots of their spines highlighted by moonlight. Their mournful song travels to me through the water and earth and reverberates up into my chest.

"I love you. Stay," I call out to them. "Don't leave me."

The whales pay no attention and slip down into the mystery of the deep. I only wish to be surrounded by all those I love, have ever loved. To have one of them wrap a blanket around my shoulders and sit with me and listen to the ocean. But all my loved ones are ghosts who rarely come to me. My parents, dead. My siblings, dead. Same with old school mates, taken away by cancers, accidents, overdoses, suicide. All eaten by this world.

I start to cry because there's no one left, all ashes and graveyards, and here I am with zero accomplishments beyond the avoidance of death, so far. How is this so? My own body, how I hate it. How it has failed me—knees that ache, a back that will not bend. It is impossible to know when you're young how the days will slip by and take your strength and vitality. Now here I am on this goddamn rock, with my face in my hands. Crying over things that just won't stop. Crying because of things that are gone, lost to what I don't even know. If I had any balls I'd jump off this cliff and end it. But I get up, wipe my face, and head back to the shelter. My cave calls to me, and I want to be within its protective walls as soon as I can. I want to be out of the sky's gaze, no longer allow it to look down on me, study me, judge me.

I step into the shack, and there's Roy with a knife high in the air over Fern's head. His eyes appear unfocused, but his intent seems clear—Fern, with a book on her lap and her attention on its pages. I step into the space between them.

"Son," I say and place my hand on Roy's shoulder.

He turns to me and blinks. I can tell he doesn't see me for who I am.

I place a hand around the wrist of his raised arm, and he glances up at his hand and the knife. I turn, and there's Fern, her eyes now also on the knife.

"Go," I command her.

She hops up and dashes out into the night. I gently remove the knife from Roy's grip and then let go of him and place the knife on a high shelf. When I go back to Roy, he's on the ground, still as a rock. I lean down next to him and rest a hand on his shoulder.

"I'm drowning," he says.

"I know," I say and ask no questions.

He begins to cry, and I take him down into the cave. Perhaps the protection of the earthen walls will help heal him too. We sob as if we may never be able to stop.

ROY

We are tracked from the moment of our birth; numbers are given, birth certificates; boxes are ticked off on charts, eye colour, weight, etc... All our peculiarities on paper. We grow and go to school, where they continue to note our development. Roy plays well with others but needs to try harder at his school work. Then we are given more numbers, Social Insurance Numbers, and Driver's Licence numbers. All these numbers in data banks, waiting to be used against us. Numbers that turn into the government's sticky fingers.

Thomas sits on the floor, his teeth sunk into one knee. I look into his eyes and know he is in some far off place.

"Thomas," I say. "Thomas, do you want to be free?"

His face swivels up. "Yes," he says.

"I know how," I say and hold my wallet in front of his distant eyes. "I'm going to burn all my ID."

"Of course," he says. "I want to be free too."

"Get everything with your name on it," I tell him. "We'll start fresh after the collapse."

Thomas tries to push himself up and falls over onto his side. With another attempt, he forces himself up onto his knees and finally stands. He grabs a small pine box, and we head up to the surface.

We go to the cliffs, and I build a fire. I stoke the wisps of flame with twigs and dry moss. My art school identification card is the first thing I set down onto the embers. The laminate bubbles and turns black. The coarse dots that meld together into an image of my face turn into a dark pool of nothingness.

"It's these things that make us conform," I say. "That's what they want. They want us to be like everyone else, to be a cog in the system."

Thomas, seated on the dirt, slouches over onto his side and sets the pine box on the ground in front of him. He opens the lid and picks up the first card, then puts it back in the box. He digs further under the contents and lifts out a school photograph of his daughter. He studies the image, and tears begin to roll down his cheeks.

"Burn the box," he says. "I want to be free."

I pick up the box and place it in the flames. We watch intently as the fire starts to bite into the shellac and then the wood. Sparks float up toward the night sky.

"Am I free yet?" Thomas asks.

I don't answer him. He's the only one who can determine his own freedom. Pine smoke hangs heavy in the air. Out on the water, distant facets of the ocean slip back and forth. I can't watch a man cry, at least not this silent version of release. He won't even wipe his face.

I hear someone singing in the woods and strain to hear what direction it might be coming from. I try to place the lyrics, but before I can recall the song the sound fades away to nothing. I'm left with Thomas' quiet sobs and the crackle of fire. I turn my attention back to the woods. Up on a slight slope, between the trees, there's a figure in a white gown.

"Fern," I call out. I want it so badly to be her. For her to come to me and run her hand down the side of my face, to unravel and re-braid my hair. I imagine my hands along the inside of her thighs. I get up and call out again, but the apparition doesn't respond. When I get closer to the figure, the white form slips behind the trees, but I keep walking toward it.

"Hello," I say to the night. "Are you there?"

I turn back for a moment. The fire has become a dim spec. The outline of Thomas' shoulder is just visible.

"It's Cedar," I hear a voice say.

"Cedar," I say out loud. "Why are you here?"

"Who knows," she says.

"I was hoping you were Fern," I say.

She gazes at the ground, her long hair framing her face. She's quite beautiful.

"Can I put my hands on your hips?" I say.

"Sure," she says.

I take my hands and graze her ghostly white robe and press until the firmness of her body stops me. "I just need to touch someone," I say.

"I understand," she says.

"Can you kiss me as if you were Fern?" I say. "Can you kiss me as if you loved me deeply?"

"I guess I can," she says.

We lean in toward each other, and I feel her lips press against mine and her tongue in my mouth. I say her name, Fern. I press the small of her back, and I feel love within me. We pull away from each other, and I reel with the universe as it bursts in my chest.

"Is that love?" she says.

"Yes," I say.

She gazes over at what's left of the fire for a moment, and then turns back to me. "I'm going to go now," she says.

"Wait. What song were you singing?"

"*It Ain't Me, Babe*," she says. "You know, Bob Dylan."

"That's it. I couldn't place the melody. Why are you singing it?"

"I don't know," she says and looks again at the ground. "I used to hear it at Dad's studio when I was a kid. I always thought it was such a cruel song in a way. You know what I mean?"

"I guess," I say.

"Tell Fern, I miss her," Cedar says.

"Do you know her?"

Cedar turns her attention to the dark of the woods and says she has to go. I wish she wouldn't, but I don't stop her. I stay until nothing of her white robe can be seen, and then I'm standing by myself. A fierce feeling of loneliness sweeps over me, and I wonder if the encounter I just had was even real. I go back and sit with Thomas, still gazing at the photograph of his poor junkie daughter, tears wet on his cheeks. Fern's kiss tingles on my lips; her love is so great, it can travel through the night, over mountains, and oceans, and come to me through other beings. That's how powerful Fern is.

CHARLES

I pencil a rudimentary female form and enjoy my coffee along with the silence of the hovel. With a fine number thirty-two filbert of hog bristle in hand, I start to contemplate colour, when a knock at the door stirs me from my reverie. I know it must be someone unfamiliar or they wouldn't knock. I go to the door and call out for whoever is on the other side to name themselves.

"It's Garth," I hear.

Christ, Garth. My day now ruined for sure; I open the door. "Have you sold some of my paintings?" I say.

"I'm looking for Roy," he says.

"Roy? Whatever for?"

He steps into the hovel and lights a cigarette. His hands appear feminine with their thin skin and long delicate fingers, like the legs of a spider.

"I sold some of his paintings."

I push the bristles of the paintbrush, still in my hand, into a plug of black oil paint, and mash the hairs in deep. Black soaks up between the bristles and under the ferrule. I will not entertain Garth with my thoughts on what he's just told me. I will not allow him to get under my skin. "Who knows where he is. Hopefully run off a cliff, but I will be sure to tell him you stopped by," I say.

But I see his attention is not on me but on the letter from my daughters, stabbed against the post.

"What's this?" he says.

"A joke," I say.

"You should take them up on it."

"Never. They are trying to ruin me."

"How?" he says.

"How?" I call out. "They want to ruin my career and destroy my masterpiece."

"I'd take them up on it. Your paintings aren't selling anymore. Take a few years off."

"Take a few years off and then what?"

"Maybe the market will change. Your art has gone out of vogue. Change your style," he says.

"Style," I cry out. "A master doesn't just change his style."

"Picasso did, Mondrian did."

"But Charles Tindal does not."

"Listen, Charles, I'm going to give you some hard facts on your art. You're a local player. Your work isn't selling in LA, New York, or even Toronto. Buyers now find your style dated, the figures too angular, the pallet too muted. People want what's new. They want something that makes a big statement. They want a Brian Jungen mask on their wall."

"Who's Brian Jungen?"

"Native guy, makes masks out of Nike running shoes."

"Jesus. I can do native."

"No, you can't."

"Bill Reid did."

"He was Haida."

"Great art isn't about what people want on their walls."

"Sure," Garth says. "But making money is."

—

The letter taunts me, jeers at me from across the room. I tear it away from the post and crush it into a ball. I will not be blackmailed by them. I squeeze the ball in my fist and release my grip when the small oil painting that leans against my brushes catches my attention. The paint is cracked and yellowed with age. The image is of a pigeon, grey and dull, but there's something that appeals to the eye, perhaps the symmetry. My father dabbled in art and produced this specimen when I was a child. He must have thought something of what he accomplished because he gave this one small painting to me as a gift for my ninth birthday. Somehow, it has survived all my moves and travels. I pick up the canvas, hold it aloft, and study the places where the paint thickens and thins. In the bottom right-hand corner are his initials. On the back of the painting, the soft underbelly of the canvas is darkened with age. I can't help but wonder why the painting exists? Why a pigeon? Why the gift? He was fond of birds and plants that unfurled from the earth in the damp and dreary early days of spring. But did pigeons, in particular, mean something to him? I'll never know.

The rabbit hole my thoughts slip down into exposes new emotions, irritation, and then anger. I take the letter and the pigeon painting and leave the hovel, as if the place itself is part of the problem. It's dark, but I feel my way along the path that leads out through the forest to the cliffs. Garth's words spin in my head. If my art doesn't sell in Toronto, New York or LA, shouldn't the blame be placed at his feet? A problem with the representation as opposed to the art? I've seen these fresh talents, with their canvases of dots and lines, grotesque enlarged faces. I ask myself, has great literature gone out of style? Is no one reading Nabokov or Dostoyevsky?

I think I hear the voices of my daughters in song, and I freeze statue-still on the trail. I strain to catch any sound that might emerge from the undergrowth, curious as to what song they might choose. But all I hear is the distant break of ocean on the beach and the rustle of fir trees and the strange throb of life that courses through my body. I take a step forward, still with the belief that they might be out there. I haven't seen or heard them since they assaulted me with their pen. I continue along the trail, taut for any sound that might emerge from the forest. Up ahead there's a glow, close to the ground. I draw near to find a fire and a body on the ground. Closer yet, I discover it is Thomas, the poor sod.

I take a seat on a low stump. "Hello, old friend," I say.

He doesn't move, but his eyes flicker in my direction.

"Have you heard, my daughters are trying to destroy me for once and all?" I say. Again, he remains silent. Bored, I stand up and toss the balled-up letter onto the sad fire. Flames burst to life, turning the edges bright orange and then black.

"I'd take the offer," Thomas says.

So he can speak. Actual words have come out of his mouth.

"I'd do anything for my daughter," he says and shows me her sad school picture.

"Anything but stay clean," I say.

His face drops, and his eyes close. "Anything but that," he says.

I decide I'll retake my seat on the stump and enjoy whatever warmth the fire has to give. I study the small canvas, the white of the pigeon's eye leers at me.

"Were you burning something?" I say, unsure I'll get any response.

"Our IDs," he says.

The 'our' includes Roy I suspect. "Splendid idea," I say. "There is nothing more cleansing than a good fire."

More silence from my companion.

"ID is like a prison," I say. "Used by the government to track you. I will not be their monkey."

Thomas is mute with his eyes closed and half of his face in the dirt. I assume he's still breathing.

"We should burn all things. There is no room for sentimentality," I say and toss the canvas into the fire. The flames crack and burst and turn the oil paint into a heavy black smoke. The single eye of the pigeon remains fixed on me until the flames reach the spec of titanium white, and then that too is gone. I stand up and knock the dust off my pant legs. "I feel lighter already," I say and take a step toward the hovel.

"I'd do anything," Thomas says.

"Sure," I say and continue to walk away, my thoughts on the search for a new art dealer.

THOMAS

I pull apart all the things that belong to me and decide that I'll begin to shed myself of all excess. At the bottom of a cardboard box, full of music tapes and photographs, I find a small handgun. God knows why I've held onto any of this. I take the box out to the cliffs and one by one throw the pictures out into the void. Black and white images of my childhood that I cleanse myself of. If there are no pictures, then it must not have happened. Blurry images of me as a small boy in a cowboy outfit with a six-shooter held tight in my pudgy fist. One lone photograph of my mother. She's thin and has her hands in the pockets of her dress; her back rests against a door frame. I take one last look at her face and toss the photograph into the nothingness, to be eaten by the sea. The photograph cuts back and forth through the air until it falls out of view.

My heart lightens with each image that flutters out over the waves and gets pulled down into the depths. This is what has held me down, this box of the past. Then I pick up the gun, hard and solid in my hand, and place the barrel to my temple, contemplating the feel of the hard metal against thin skin and hard skull. I don't know why there are threads in me that cling to life, that cling to crawling forward. I don't know why. I envy those who can just end it all. Perhaps they're the strongest we have. I hurl the gun out into the air. It spins and drops through space until it too is out of view. For a moment I want to chase after it, run off the cliff and follow its trajectory. If I survived the fall, then finally I would use that gun for what was always its intended purpose.

When the box is empty, I toss it too over the cliff and go back to the shelter empty-handed.

ROY

I walk to the road and stick my thumb out in hopes that someone will give me a ride to town. Two young guys pick me up and offer to smoke a joint with me, which I can't pass up. They're surf boarders, they say, from Australia, come to surf the waves off Vancouver Island. Their weed is strong, so much so that I can barely remember why I got into their car. Then it comes back to me—I want to call my mom. The guys drop me off in front of an appliance repair shop, and I cross the street to a diner to ask if I can use their phone. They tell me there's a payphone down the road. Jerks. I pull down a string of tacky gold-coloured garland, hung low over the top of the door frame, as I leave.

The pay phone has a door that doesn't close and busted out panes of glass. I dial the operator and say I want to make a collect call. There are clicks and popping sounds, and then my mother's voice, which I wish didn't send me down a spiral of being four, then eight, then twelve. How I wish the number took me to someone else's mother. A mother, kind and eager to listen. For some reason, I begin to cry, a real cry with gasps and sobs. There's snot and tears and a white-hot burn in my chest.

"What do you want?" she says.

And I have to wonder myself, what is it that I want? To wind back the clock and start over, to be birthed again into this world, fresh, untainted, unmolested. I want things that are impossible. I want things she can in no way provide me, even if she wanted to.

"There's a storm coming," I sputter into the phone.

"Good God, Roy. What is this? You on drugs?"

"No Mom!" I yell. "No, I'm not on drugs." I slam the receiver into the pay phone box over and over until the black plastic cracks. When I stop, the receiver is limp, like a broken doll in two halves. Only the wires, like intestines, hold the pieces together.

"Mom!" I scream into the dead phone, into a black pit of silence.

I walk for miles back toward the trailhead, dragging my feet through the gravel. Vehicles don't even slow down when I stick my thumb out. She failed you, runs through my head like a broken record. She failed you. This is what Fern says when the subject of my mom comes up. She failed you. You did not fail her; she failed you. This is what I wanted to tell her on the phone. You failed me. You failed me and always made me feel it was the other way around. It was you, not me.

It starts to rain. How perfect for my mood. Wind swirls up around me. By the time I get to the trail, I decide to strip myself of all worldly possessions. I'll live as a hermit. I take off my shirt and throw it into the forest, then my shoes and pants. I'm a wild man, with no connections or needs. The forest floor and sea will provide my sustenance. Trees will act as my mother and protector. Finally, I've shed everything that weighed me down. I climb over fallen trees and take handfuls of wild berries. I find thin little mushrooms to eat, and soon I feel my head swoop and spin. My hands turn into paws, and I become a wolf. I climb up into my watchtower, where I howl and howl at the moonless night sky.

Sometime during the night, I think I hear the soft hush of a woman's voice sing that Neil Young song, *Old Man*. A song I thought was being sung by a woman when I was a child. The lyrics call to me, and I climb down from the watchtower to prowl among my mother trees, and my sisters and brothers, who grow beside them.

—

Warmth surrounds me as if I have climbed into a bear's den. There are flickers of sound, strange clicks, and hushed voices. A woman with a cherub-like face and long black hair appears above me and then is gone. There's the smell of food. I open my eyes and find myself in a bed with a thick blanket over my body. The room is small, with photos on the walls of people I don't know. I stay quiet and wait.

A woman comes into the room and takes a quick look at me. "George, George," she yells. "He's awake." She leans over me.

"We thought you were dead. Don't need some white guy dying in our house."

"White," I say. "How do you know I'm white?"

"Those braids aren't fooling anyone. If you're Indian, you're not from around here," she says.

"But how do you know I'm not from here?"

"Because I know everyone here you fool. Jeesh, now I know you're white for sure. You ask dumb questions."

"I could be from the prairies."

At this she bends back, hand to stomach, and laughs, her mouth open to the sky. "Oh man, you're too much. No prairie Indian would be found in a ditch outside my house on the west coast."

Now, the guy who must be George is beside her. He appears to study me.

"This fool thinks he's a prairie Indian," she says to him.

"Oh," he says. "Are you?"

They both turn to me and wait.

"I guess not," I say.

"Are you half?" George asks.

"No," I say. "I'm nothing."

"We have some chili on the stove. Do you want some?" George says.

When I get out of the bed, I find someone has put old-man pyjamas on me. We walk through a living room where a Christmas tree is set up, decorated with multicoloured lights that blink on and off. The kitchen is homey with a breakfast nook and the heavy smell of chili and meat. A big bowl is set down in front of me with a chunk of bread.

"How did I get here?" I say.

"You were naked, crying and yelling in the ditch out front, like some lunatic," George says.

The cherub-faced woman pushes the butter toward me. "Something about wanting to see the medicine man. So we went and got Dr. Tara. You guys were in the room there for hours. Any time we put our ear to the door, all we could hear was sobbing."

"She wouldn't tell us what you guys talked about," George adds.

94

I try to think back to the night, but there's nothing but blackness.

"What are you doing out here, anyway?" George asks.

"Me and some friends are living in the woods until the world comes to an end," I say.

"Oh, when will that be?" George asks.

"New Year's Eve," I say.

George and the woman chuckle a bit. "The new year will be the same as the last," George says.

"It's going to be anarchy," I say. "Banks will close. People will riot. Airplanes will fall from the sky."

"I'll take my chances," George laughs. "How are you fools surviving in the woods?"

"I'm not sure," I say.

We eat the chili, and I take in all the photographs hung on the walls—babies, school pictures, and grandparents. It all makes me sad because I have no photographs of anybody in my family.

"This all your family?" I ask.

"Sure," George says, and he starts to tell me who's in every picture.

"Do they all live around here?" I ask.

"All of them. We're all here. My son lives next door. My parents are just down the road."

George gives me an old pair of running shoes and takes me to see his shed in the back where he says he carves masks. He shows me a new slab of cedar he just got and the mask that he's in the midst of carving. Then we go for a walk along a stream that runs behind the houses. On the way back we meet a woman with a purple jacket on.

"Hello, Roy," she says.

A strange creep of electricity runs down through the core of my body and out through my hands and feet. George must be able to tell that I don't recognize this woman. He says, "This is Dr. Tara from last night."

My knees wobble, and I slip down onto the wet path and start to sob. The sobs come up in waves like dry heaves. Dr. Tara kneels down beside me and says, "You'll have to work this all out. You'll have to cry until you can't anymore. You need to go back to where you came from. From where you originate." She stands up and nods to George, who's taken a seat on a stump, and then she walks away.

When she's gone I feel lighter. I wipe at my eyes and look over at George, who appears unsurprised by this whole display.

"What was that?" I say.

"Dr. Tara has that effect on people. If she says you need to cry more, then you need to cry. And go back to where you are from."

"I don't know where I come from."

"Maybe that's part of the problem."

We walk back to the house. I tell them I should go, and thank them for what they've done.

"What are you guys eating out there?" George asks. "Bark and kelp?"

"We have people that bring us food."

"How's that going to work when the world ends?" he says and laughs. He hands me a large plastic container full of sandwiches and fruit. "Don't worry about the container," he says. "And keep the pyjamas."

I'm on the road when George calls out my name. "I forgot," he says. "There's a storm coming. It's supposed to be a big one. You guys should reinforce your shelter."

"I know," I say and wave goodbye.

CHARLES

With my fishing line, I head out to a shear rock on the water with good depth and kelp beds. The idea is to get a rock cod for dinner. I near the intended fishing point, and out there on the cliff is a human form with the small shoulders of a woman. A part of me jumps to life with the thought of a friendly exchange of bodily warmth. But when the form comes into greater clarity, all that came to life dies, and a deep freeze sets into my bones. Blue, my middle child, sits like a hag, washed ashore on a rock. I take a quick glance around for the others. Perhaps they've plotted to push me off the edge.

"Hi," she says.

"Out here for the view?" I say.

"It's nice," she says and pans the horizon. "Do you fish often?"

"I don't make a habit of it, but the thought of fresh fish tonight was appealing." I put down my bucket, bait the hook with a piece of moss, and drop it into the water. With a wish for silence, I light a cigarette and take a seat on a rock.

"Can I have one?" she asks.

I remain still for a moment. Maybe the voice was an aberration, a trick played by the wind and lap of the sea.

"Can I have a smoke?" she asks again.

Do they think I'm made of money? I reach into my coat for the pack, hand her a single cigarette, and hope that keeps her quiet.

"Can I have a light?"

I bite my tongue, light her damn cigarette, and then give the line a few tugs. She begins to cough, deep raspy hacks that pitch her forward and then back. She beats her chest with a fist and then drops the cigarette, not even half smoked, and extinguishes it with her foot. She hangs her head in her hands and makes small sniffle sounds.

"I don't actually smoke," she says.

Good, I think, she won't waste more of my cigarettes. Then the line jolts. I take a glance off the rock ledge and begin to reel up my catch. The red spines of a snapper break the surface, small, but it'll make a tidy meal tonight. I pull the hook from its lip and drop it into the bucket. I'd normally stay and try to catch another, but the company brings me down. She scratches at her arms like she has lice and tugs on her damp hair. I gather my things, pick up the bucket, and take a step in the direction of the hovel.

"Wait," she says.

Dammit, I thought I might make a clean getaway. Already I can smell the snapper sizzling in a hot pan with butter.

"Do you want to know why we sing *California Dreaming*?"

I do not, but I have a feeling this doesn't matter. "Why?" I say.

"When I was small and I would ask mom where you were, she would always say California."

"Okay," I say. "Enjoy the view." I take a few more steps away from her, the taste of fresh snapper in my thoughts.

"Wait," she calls.

It's intolerable, like being held hostage. I feel as if I may never get away from this miserable soul.

"Why have you never asked anything about me?"

This is going to go on forever. I wish a bolt of lightning would strike me down. "What would you like me to ask?" I say, dumbfounded by her line of questioning.

"How are you? What have you been up to?" she says, and she stands, trembling. "What have you been doing for the last twenty-five years?" she yells.

"I assume you have been living your life," I say, unsure how to bring this all to a close.

She collapses back down on the rock and clasps her face in her hands. "You're such a selfish man. Miranda was right."

"Miranda. What does she have to do with this?"

"She said you're an animal. Garbage not to be bothered with."

"Miranda would not say that about her father. The bunch of you are a real sad lot." I decide I've had enough of her complaints and start to walk away. The further I get from her the better I feel. My mood improving with each step.

"You're a horrible person," she yells. "A horrible, horrible person."

I can't believe how these girls think it's okay to treat their father this way. It's quite astonishing.

ROY

In the watchtower, I eat the food from George and come up with a plan for the storm. I climb down and creep through the woods back to the shack with the idea to steal all the food and drink. I'll take it all up to the sky, so I may never have to come down again. My body tingles with the sensation of the wolf spirit that pumps through my limbs. My mouth tastes of raw meat and mud. Before I get to the shack, I sit on the cliffs and smoke half a pack of cigarettes. The air isn't clear yet of the morning mist and damp of the woods. Ahead of me is the big unknowable foreverness of the ocean. Serenity and peace wash over me. How could anything ever be better than this moment, right here, right now? Not a soul on this earth of six billion knows where I am. Not my mother, not my dead father, or my siblings, old girlfriends, teachers, the man in the headdress. I could, with one slip, fall into the Pacific and be done with it, and no one would know. My body pulled down to forever be tugged about by the deep currents on the ocean floor. I would leave my paintings to Fern. My girl would know what to do. She would work with Garth to build the legend that was Roy Kruk. Just as Tom Thomson canoed off into the sunset, I too would ascend to artistic genius in only the way a mysterious death or disappearance can foster. I unwind my braids and comb my fingers through my long black hair.

The sound of waves smashing against the rocks shakes something loose in my head. I'm a child, my father, angry, and he's dragging me through the house by my arm. The smell of cigarette smoke and wet drywall. The house always felt like it was made out of cardboard, and could dissolve into a mess of pulp every time it rained. I don't know what I've done or what's about to happen, but I know he's mad. He doesn't talk to me. He doesn't explain anything. We're in the bathroom, and he lifts me, with his rough hands, sits me down on the vanity counter. The shaver is pressed down to my scalp, pulling and twisting my hair. He slaps me, tells me to hold still, but that's what I've tried to do. I try. I'm trying. I'm trying. I try so hard to be still, to be silent, to be good. I try to be impossible.

"Fucking woman," he says.

The shaver gouges my skin. The air around me is black with hair like ash around a house fire.

Dad, dad, dad, I want to say between sobs, but my mouth doesn't work. Nothing works. I'm spit and tears and hands that reach out for my father. I think I must have been five or four. When Fern asked me what my first memory was, this is what I told her. But now that I think about it, that wasn't my first memory. My first memories are sounds and feelings. The sounds of things that slam. The sound of loud music and laughter. Laughter that sounded like the snaps and barks of wild dogs outside my bedroom window, about to break in and tear me to pieces. The sensation of my body getting tight. My arms and legs paralyzed.

I get up. For a moment I teeter on the edge of the cliff and feel the emptiness under my toes. How simple it would be to tip forward. The thrilling rush of air, streaming past my head, and then the beautiful blackness, like sleep but better. Artists never use black alone; black by itself is flat and empty. Black must be mixed with blue or red to give it depth and dimension. Black by itself is not enough. I step back and head toward the shack.

Inside the air is dank and gloomy. I go to the shelf where we keep the food and start to fill up my duffle bag. Then I raid our earthen fridge, under boards in the forest floor. There's salami, a block of cheese. I go over to my corner studio and find Fern asleep on the rug in a puddle of blankets like a fawn. I kneel over her, bury my face in her neck, and inhale her scent of light and some flowery perfume. I take handfuls of her flesh wanting to hold every part of her and push aside the blankets and clothes that have become a barrier to our togetherness. She reaches out for me with her smooth fingertips and her gentle hands. Her hair all gold and wild on the dirt floor. I always told Fern that I've never once fucked her, that what I do to her is mythic and of another realm. It's the aurora borealis. We crack apart and turn inside out like the earth on Judgment Day. I'm the wind, an eagle. I'm the bolt of light rained down on the mountains by Zeus.

"You're killing me, you're killing me," I say to her.

I grab the damp flesh behind her knees. She tips her head back and opens her mouth. Forever, all the world's beauty and joy has come from out of a woman's mouth. Like the Haida who believe the first man crawled out from between the open shell of a clam. I believe he came out from the mouth of a woman—all that beautiful moist darkness. Fern puts her arms around me and pulls me down beside her. Her chest rises and falls with the rapid beat of her heart.

"Everything, everything," she says.

I pull away damp threads of my hair from her cheek and know I will never have enough of her. That perhaps it's impossible that anyone could ever have enough of Fern. She turns her head to me and takes all of me in with her green eyes. She wipes away my tears.

"You're so broken," she says.

"I know," I say.

"There's a storm coming."

This I know too and ask if she will braid my hair.

THOMAS

My wife appears and restocks my supply.

"This will be it," I tell her. "As of New Year's I'll be clean, cold turkey."

"We should have a big family dinner," she says.

"Yes, yes, with Iris too?"

"Yes, of course with Iris." She takes out a package for me, wrapped in festive green paper and says, "Open it."

I tear away the wrapping to find a thin book, *The Wreck of the Hesperus*, by Henry Wadsworth Longfellow. I open the book and read the first few lines to myself:

It was the schooner Hesperus
That sailed the wintry sea
And the skipper had taken his little daughter
To bear him company.

I tell my wife how much I appreciate it and then give her a small wood carving I made of the three of us. Myself, my wife, and Iris, stand shoulder to shoulder. I point out the fine detail, how behind us my hand is held by her hand and how Iris' hand is held in my other.

"It's beautiful," she says.

"It'll be a wonderful dinner," I say.

"A whole new start, and a new life," she says.

When my wife is about to leave she remembers that she has a letter for me from Iris. She hands me an envelope and says she'll see me soon. When my wife is gone, I rip open the seal.

Dad

My bones are broken. They pierce my lungs and heart. The air we breathe pulls me inside out. I hate you. I hate you. I hate you.

Love,
Iris

ROY

I'm stirred from my sleep by the scamper of something below me, then a knock on the floor hatch of my watchtower.

"Roy, It's me, Fern. Let me in," you say.

I open the hatch, and you climb up into my crow's nest. You give me a small box and say, "Merry Christmas."

"Christmas," I say out loud, as if the word is new to me.

"Ya, Christmas dummy. Open your gift."

I take the box and lift the cardboard lid off. Inside is a chain and a pendant of some clear crystal.

You pick up the chain and place it over my head. "It's selenite. It's a healing crystal."

"What does it heal?" I ask.

"Everything. It will help guide you home."

I hold the crystal in my palm, and tears fill my eyes.

"You don't have to cry," you say.

I turn and grab one of my eagle feathers and hand it to you. "Take it," I say.

You take the feather and give me a kiss. "I know you don't like Christmas."

"It's a bunch of bullshit."

"I know," you say. "Listen, I have to leave the woods for a bit, but I'll be back for New Year's Eve."

I pepper you with questions. Where are you going? Why are you leaving? Who will you be with? All of my questions are met with vague answers.

I insist I walk you to the edge of the forest, and on the walk the thought builds and builds in my head that you're about to slip out of my grasp. I imagine this is inevitable; after all, everything I've ever coveted has ended in ruin. From what little safety and comfort I had as a child to my father who took his own life. Small threads I tried to hang onto, always eventually, unraveled and broke. Women, in whose eyes I have found sun-filled meadows which later turned into charred earth. You haven't said as much, but there's been a rupture, glances off into the distance, shifts away from my touch. You walk with steady determination to get to the outside world, always a few steps ahead of me. When we step out of the forest and into the open, I'm surprised to find how bright the day is.

"Don't leave me," I say to you.

"I'll be back before the storm hits with food and stuff," you say.

You're all business, and I know you haven't heard me. "No," I say. "Don't leave me." I take your hand and place it on my chest, over my heart.

"I will eventually," you say.

Light opens up around you and picks up the copper in your hair. Your expression gives nothing away. I know what you say is true, but I'd like to imagine it's one of your quirky toss-away comments, which you're known for.

"When you come back, I'll paint you," I say.

"Sure," you say, but now I wonder if you'll really come back at all. Perhaps this is it. I slip down onto the gravel, my arms wrapped around your legs, my face pressed into your thighs. You're so still that I want to scream, force a reaction. I want you to scream back, kick, and bite, tell me what a terrible person I am and all the things I've ever done wrong.

"I'll be back in a few days," you say.

I snicker and then laugh, not even sure what emotion I'm trying to demonstrate. "Superman reversed the rotation of the earth, and turned back time to save Lois Lane."

"Are you Superman now?" you say with a hint of a smile. "Michelangelo isn't enough?"

"What is ever enough?" I say.

There's no answer from you. You walk away and get into your car, and then you're gone.

—

I have no real faith. I believe in no deities or spirits. Jehovah himself has excommunicated me. All I have is you, Fern, and my art. When I go back to the shack, Charles and Thomas are in some argument about who is currently the world's greatest living artist, Hurst, or Koons. Neither of them, I say. All their work is bullshit. I go back to the watchtower and twist the cap off a fresh mickey of rum. That first drink is like fireworks in my chest. I sketch image after image of you. I stab the paper with deep gouges to form the silhouette of your hip. I take another drink, then smudge in the fine detail of your ankles. Each drawing grows cruder and cruder, like Schiele and his whores. Legs spread wide to taunt and make a man trip over his toes. I rip each drawing free of the pad and send it off into the void over the forest canopy.

I have no god. The man in the headdress told me to get down on my knees and opened his Bible to share the good word of Jehovah. How I could be one of the saved. How I could see paradise earth with the chosen. To be saved was what I wanted more than anything. For once, to be wanted, to be special. He showed me the pictures of what paradise looked like, with its green lush grass and people infused with the light of righteousness. All that beautiful light. Just like the Lawren Harris painting, *Houses in Richmond Street*. You wouldn't believe how beautiful a painting of a house could be. All that light and beauty and promise, but when you move close, it falls apart—the illusion loosens and dissipates.

I tear at the paper and stab the sheets with my pencil over and over again until the lead and wood splinters. I have no animal spirit or totem to pull from. I only have you, and look what you're doing to me. Look how you treat me when all I've done is love you. I scream your name into the winds that have started to swirl around the tops of the trees. I scream your name until it feels as if my throat is bleeding.

Once, when I was a child, a charity dropped off a food basket on our step for Christmas Eve. I studied everything inside, through its cellophane barrier. I watched that basket while I ate my hotdog dinner. I watched the basket until a smack from Mom announced that it was bedtime. In the morning I got up and went straight to the kitchen. There was the basket, all its contents ravaged. I picked up empty boxes of what must have been tasty treats to find not even a scrap left behind.

The medicine woman told me to go home, back to where I came from.

CHARLES

At the hovel, I find Miranda, my oldest, seated on a stump beside the front door.

"Where are your muckraking siblings?" I ask her.

"Gone into town," she says.

No doubt to get some type of poison for their papa. "Are you here to cause your old man grief?" I say.

"I'm sure my very existence causes you grief," she responds.

"I suppose you want to come in, or something." I open the door for her to follow me inside. Thankfully there's no one else there. Where they've gone off to, I don't know, nor do I care. With Roy and Thomas and especially Fern off somewhere else, there's the promise of solitude and space for my mind to be consumed with my art. I boil coffee grounds and hand a mug to Miranda. She seats herself on one of the floor pillows and studies my masterwork.

"What do you think?" I ask her.

"About what?"

"The painting of course."

She takes a lazy glance at the canvas and then a sip of coffee. "Is it one of yours?" she says.

"Of course it's mine. It could be no other. It carries all my signature techniques. See the angular edges of the forms?"

"I guess it's okay. It's not really my kind of thing."

Can you imagine this insufferable woman who spouts off like this about her own father's painting? Would she say this about a Rembrandt? It's really not my thing. Any patience I might have had for her evaporates.

"What brings you this way?" I say, but really mean to ask, should you not be on your way?

"Mom kept clippings of everything on you, gallery shows, interviews, things like that."

"And so she should. I'm sure my fame boosted her morale."

"No, it wasn't for that. She said she kept it all so I would know who my father was."

"I'm right here. Do you not know me?"

"But I didn't want them. I read through the articles, but they made me angry, so I threw them all out. It seemed like complete bullshit."

"Bullshit? What do you mean?"

"All those articles made you sound important. Like you were someone worth knowing," she says.

Jesus, this girl. "What are you getting at?" I say.

"But I knew better. I knew what a weak, empty spirit you actually are," she says.

"You're out of your mind," I say to her.

"Don't you think it's important to hear what your daughter thinks? Wouldn't you want to know what type of article your daughter would write about you."

"No," I say and laugh. "No one would care what you have to say. What harm have I done to you?"

"Perhaps I'd start by saying how little I actually know, that all my observations are collected from the very few times we've actually been together."

"Your mother has poisoned your view on me."

"Actually, she never said much of anything. She said you were a painter of postcard scenes."

"She what?" I stammer. "Look at this canvas. It is no postcard."

She points at me with an accusatory finger. "Remember the times I came to your openings, and you ignored me?"

"I hardly ignored you. I was at work."

"As much as I wanted to know you, it was impossible."

"Is this it? You have just come here to gripe and moan, to knock your poor father down?"

"I've come here to tell you what it was like to be one of your daughters. To be the unspoken-of-daughter of the great Charles Tindal. The master expressionist of the West Coast. Charles Tindal, the raconteur, the man who rubbed shoulders with the beats, the man who romanced a kaleidoscope of women, who dined with celebrities," she says.

"Do tell," I say. "I would love to hear it."

"It was shit," she spits.

"You've got nothing to do with it," I say. "What is all that to you?"

"What's all that to me?" she yells and gets up on her feet.

At this point, I hope someone shows up, Roy, or Charles, even Fern. I don't know what's gotten her so riled.

"I wanted you!" she yells and shakes her fists like a child. She wipes her nose on her sleeve and says, "Thank God for Cory."

My insides turn black, and whatever humour and patience I might have had for this situation leaves me entirely. Now I just want her gone, no more fanfare or grandstanding on her part. What am I to do? Take her in my arms and tell her what a wonderful person she is, pet her hair? This is exactly why children aren't needed in the studio with their endless disturbances. My nerves are shot today. How will I get any painting done? Then something surfaces about her last comment. "Who's Cory?" I say.

"He's my stepdad," she snorts with a tone that implies I'm supposed to know this.

"Stepdad?" I repeat.

"You know? The guy that mom married when I was a kid?"

"Cory? What kind of name is that for a man? Maybe you can take your troubles to him?" I suggest.

"Oh my god, I hate you so much," she says and scoops up a fistful of paintbrushes. Before I can stop her she hurls them at my masterwork. Brushes spray out through the air and bounce off the canvas, each then clatters to the floor. I'd rather she kick me in the balls or stab me in the chest.

I dive toward the canvas and frantically try to assess what damage there might be. "You wretched brat," I say, scouring my painting for damage. There's one small indent in a particularly thick swath of paint. Already my thoughts have swung to how this can work to my benefit, how this will make a wonderful story for the work when placed on the market. Familial turmoil. It worked for Picasso. When I turn away from the painting, I find Miranda is no longer there, the door left wide open. I go to close the door and find, at the threshold, a piece of rose quartz. I pick the quartz up and take a look out into the forest, but there appears to be no one there.

THOMAS

Idle hands are the devil's tool, that's what my mother used to say, and now I believe her. I decide we need lumber to patch walls on the shelter, reinforcement for the expected storm. Out in the woods, I find a manageable tree to fell and start to hack at its bark with an axe. I'm no woodsman, so it's slow and sloppy work, but I keep at it, and eventually the tree decides it no longer has the will to stand. The trunk plummets to the ground with an unexpected violence. I begin to strip the trunk of branches but soon get hot and decide to open one of the beers I brought. The combination of exerted effort and beer causes me to grow drowsy. I find a soft spot amongst the boughs of the felled tree and drift off.

Something wet on my face starts to wake me. I smooth my hand over my cheeks and feel moisture. There's a giggle that sounds like my daughter. I open my eyes, and above me there's a black shape of someone who blocks the sun's light. The rays bend and glow around the head like a halo.

"Iris," I say.

"Dad," she says.

I sit up and rest my back against the tree trunk. "Iris, what are you doing here?"

"I came to see you." She lowers to the ground and puts her arms around me.

I hold her firm, "It's good to see you kiddo." At arm's length, I study her. "You look good," I say and mean it. There's a brightness to her complexion. Her usually rail-thin frame has filled out in a healthful way. Her eyes, which are always like looking into a mirror, appear happy. I pull her to me again and hold her. "How has so much time passed?" I say. "How is such a beautiful creature, my daughter? I don't deserve it."

"Mom says you're going clean."

"Yes. I am. In fact, I already have."

"Really?"

"Yes."

"Me too," she says. "I'm clean."

My heart wants to explode with relief.

"I miss you," she says.

"I miss you too," I say.

We sit in the quiet of the forest, and I hold her hand. Waves break on the beach in the distance. There are a few sharp caws of a raven.

"I'm sorry for any pain I caused you," I say.

"It's okay Dad. I'm sorry for all the trouble I caused."

"Iris," I say. "You haven't caused any trouble." Then I tell her all about my life. I tell her about the small town where I was born and grew up. I even tell her about the shadow. I tell her how I've run away from almost everything in my life and how I hurt people and most of all how my greatest regret is hurting her.

"It's okay Dad," she says.

"No, it's not. No child should be so forgiving. You're too good for this earth." I ask her to tell me all the ways I've hurt her.

She pushes her hair back behind her ears, scoops it up in one lock and braids it, just like her mother does. She tells me about when she was small and always felt an emptiness in her stomach and feared almost everything—the dark, the school bus, other kids. She had unexplained visions of her parents vanishing, house fires, and car accidents. Cataclysmic weather events stormed in her mind. She chewed her fingernails until they bled, and she clawed at her flesh. All these things she carried into the world. A world she struggled to navigate.

A tear slips down her cheek, and I wipe it away. I look into her damp eyes and I say, sorry, sorry a thousand times over. "The woods have given me so much time to think about our life. When I leave here we're going to be together for the rest of our lives, and I'll do everything I can to be the father you should have had."

"It's okay. You were a good dad," she says.

"You don't have to lie. I know that isn't true." I ask her what her ambitions are, and she tells me she wants to be a writer.

"Iris, you'll be an amazing writer. Imagine the tales you could tell. When we're home I'll build you a writing desk."

"That would be nice," she says.

"Do you have some of your writing with you?"

"No. But I can come back with it."

"Please do," I say.

"Dad," Iris says. "When I was younger, I didn't have the words to tell you how much I loved you. Or what it felt like to love you. But now I can try. The love I feel is like being encased in wet concrete that is slowly drying. And I can feel the space in my lungs become less and less and my arms and legs begin to harden. Does that make sense?"

"Yes," I say. "I feel the same way."

"Do you remember once, when I was small, you came into my room at night and woke me up? And you said we are all children experiencing our worst day."

"No. I'm sorry. I don't remember," I say.

"I think about that a lot," she says and then stands up. "I have to go, but I'll come back later with my writing."

I push myself up onto my feet. My bones and muscles do not want to agree. I hold Iris tight and tell her again how sorry I am and how much I love her.

"It's okay Dad. I'm glad you're going clean."

"For you," I say. "It'll be a great new year."

"It will," she says.

I watch her until the last vestiges of her pink shirt fade into the dark of the forest.

ROY

A flash so bright strikes me, and I know exactly what needs to be done; I must create a manifesto. All great movements had one. Perhaps this is what I've needed all this time. I run to the shack, barely able to breathe and filled with what I must get onto paper. Charles is in rapture with his God-awful painting and takes no notice of me.

With a pen and a large sheet of my best vellum, I rush back to the watchtower. The energy around me is so fierce I almost expect the forest floor to explode with fire or bolts of lightning to shoot from trees. It must be the crystal. Perhaps Fern is right about it. Of course she is. Fern is right about everything. I climb up the tree and pull myself into the crow's nest of the watchtower. I light a joint, pace the floor, and tap the pen against my teeth.

"Authenticity!" I yell. "Yes, authenticity."

Greatness can come from nothing else. On the sheet of vellum I write, "Authenticity above all else." I'm so bold. I'm so great. My body throbs with life, like the sun burns. Yes, my mind is brilliantly clear. Why have I not done this earlier? And then I write, "Craft your mythology."

I inhale the last of the joint and then light a cigarette and sit still for a moment, my eyes closed. I've always seen myself as a man of the soil, of the deep dark heart of the forest. A man of majesty in black and white, my hair braided, the sunset behind me.

Then I write, "Destroy what gets in your way." This may be the greatest rule. There will be those who plot to take you down. Those who will deceive. They must be felled. And then for the last rule I write, "Set your price." I sit back and read this last point a few times and roll the words around in my mouth like marbles. As every artist knows, if the art doesn't sell, shit on it and then raise the price.

I yell out over the Pacific, "Yes, yes, yes!"

I will command the highest prices. I will break records. I can hear the sound of the auctioneer's gavel now and the cheers of the crowd.

A gust of wind smashes up against my shelter and sends me off balance. I reach out for the wall of the crow's nest, to steady myself. I gaze out over the horizon and notice thick black clouds have started to gather.

CHARLES

Fern arrives with some soft-skinned kid named Shane. He has a lousy grin and elastic limbs. She says he's a "friend" and that he wants to meet Thomas. I notice their flirtatious exchanges, little touches and winks.

"Why?" I ask.

"He's famous," the kid says, like this is somehow an answer to my question.

When the kid sets eyes on Thomas, you'd think he just met the Pope or perhaps God himself.

"Mr DeWolf," the kid says. He does what looks like an awkward curtsy and shakes Thomas' hand.

Thomas, who has spent most of the day seated in the corner with his head on his knees and his back rounded like a tortoise, barely responds.

"It's so amazing to meet you," the kid says.

Thomas' knees shift to one side, and he lifts his chin. "Sure," is all he can muster.

"I can't believe you're here man," the kid blabbers. "In the woods and all. Don't you have like a fortune stashed somewhere? You should be living in luxury in South America or something."

"You've seen too many movies," Thomas replies.

"But you've done so many amazing things. Like, haven't you robbed over fifty banks?"

Thomas shakes his head and closes his eyes, as if he's fallen into a coma. "It was unintentional," he says and opens his eyes. He digs into a pocket on the inner lining of his jacket and pulls out a tin box with a needle and spoon, sets up to cook, and shoot, as if we weren't there.

The kid, undeterred, lights a cigarette. "Wasn't there a movie made about you?"

Thomas lifts his chin from where it nested on his breastbone. "None of them are true."

"What do you mean?" the kid says.

"Are people pillaging out there? Are there food shortages?" Thomas asks.

"No," the kid says. "Why?"

"The world is coming to an end."

"Ha. Ya, nothing is happening yet. I guess we have a few days before the world falls apart."

The kid assaults Thomas with more questions. I turn my back to it all and continue with my canvas. If the kid had any sense he'd ask me about my art. But I see how Thomas attracts the low attention of the youth. I can hear Thomas tell the kid how he's going cold turkey New Year's Day. The kid's probably just stupid enough to believe him.

THOMAS

In my cave I shoot up and try to shake the look and inquiries of that boy, Shane. His eyes were on me as if I was someone worth his worship. How I should have told him, my life has been a waste, I've been a coward, and a fraud. I should have told him how I've broken people, myself included. I should have told that boy to go to school, to become someone productive, to become a help not a hindrance. But I told him no such thing. Coward.

Above me, I can hear Charles rant about the government and how he's convinced he's under surveillance. For what reason I can't imagine. He slams things to the floor and against the walls. There's the smash of glass, an ashtray perhaps. There's no end to the madness that rages above me.

Fern told us a storm is expected, the storm of the century; and I wonder of which century. Every storm now is the storm of the century. There are no layers to the immediacy or categorization of devastation. Everything is—all live, or all die. You make your choice.

I take *Tropic of Cancer* off the shelf, open the book to a random page and read what's there before me. The words rise and swim through my mind. I could eat these words. I want to become the words. I want to be in my cave forever with my books and absorb everything they might have to tell me. I let *The Wreck of the Hesperus* fall open and read the first stanza I see:

> *"Come hither! come hither, my little daughter,*
>   *And do not tremble so;*
> *For I can weather the roughest gale,*
>   *That ever wind did blow."*

I close the book and meditate on those words and tell myself that I'll read these words to Iris when I'm clean and we're all together. Then a darker thought enters my consciousness. I was just a boy when the shadow introduced me to heroin. I try to push the thoughts away and the numbness they bring to my body, but the numbness overwhelms. The shadow knew things I didn't.

Upstairs there's a crash, and then Charles yelling something. What he's on about, I don't know. Not a thing can touch me here in my cave. I close my eyes and remember a time in the pool with my girlfriend in California. Those long warm twilights when the world was perfect. A beautiful memory can be just as painful as a bad memory, just as painful as the worst memory. A memory that you know you can never get back to. A memory like a movie from someone else's life.

And Iris. Beautiful Iris, born a month premature; I didn't witness her come into the world or her first gasp for air. My wife always says, she was the girl who couldn't wait. Her questions started at an alarmingly young age. Too many questions. Why does the grass grow even though we step on it? Are there dogs in other countries? Where are you going, Dad? Dad, where have you been? Will we always be together? I close my eyes. My mind swims in a drug induced tropical ocean. The consumption of more drugs is the only way I can stay in this calm warm sea.

Someone stomps on the hatch above me.

Charles yells, "Your daughter is here and wants to see you."

No, I cannot see Iris. Sweat breaks out all over my body, and I search for somewhere to curl up. I'll get the spoon and dig deeper into the earth, maybe to the molten core. There's another bang on the hatch above.

"Thomas, Iris is here," Charles yells out.

"No," I say and then yell, "No, no, no. Go away." I can't see Iris like this. I shoot more hot liquid into my veins. The bangs and voices soften to a distant thrum, until finally there's only silence, beautiful silence.

I'm a child, asleep on the backseat of the car as Mom and Dad drive home late at night from a party. The windows are open, and Mom sings under her breath to the song on the radio. The night air is soft and sweet over my face. There's the pull of strange turns and swerves and splashes of light and darkness. Then the bump-bump of the tires rolling over the gravel ridge into our driveway, and the car stops. Mom picks me up and carries me to bed. She kisses my forehead. I want to reach out and grab her wrist so she won't leave me, but I don't because I'm supposed to be asleep. I don't want her to leave, but she does, and then I'm alone in my dark room. Alone.

Then there's an image of Iris in my damaged brain. Her hands cover her eyes, and she cries and cries. I know what I'll see even before she moves her hands away, but it doesn't alleviate the shock when she reveals the empty black sockets and tears of blood.

A blast of sound wakes me in my dark cave. A sound as if a mountain has let go and buried us in mud and rock. I climb up to the surface and find Charles is frantic. Above, a large part of the roof is completely gone, and gusts of rain pour into the shelter. The trees sway back and forth like the pendulum of a metronome gone mad. Their wet trunks, lit by periodic flashes of light, play like spooks in the dark. Charles tries to cover his canvas with blankets. He yells instructions out to the room, but there's no one else there.

"The storm is coming," Charles hollers. "The storm is going to take it all."

ROY

All night, I rage and cry and howl at the wind as it increases in velocity. All night, I threaten to eat the world. To smash the eyes out of children and the old. To rip out my heart and lungs. No one would be able to imagine the depth of my violence. The vastness of my fury. I climb down my tree and prowl through the forest. I eat mushrooms and search for grubs. There's something that tracks me. It hides behind trees and ducks behind boulders and mossy knolls. I know it's there, and I know it wants my blood. For a while I think it's Charles, finally ready to knock me off, to destroy the competition. Then I realize it's something much more evil.

I head down to the beach and douse my naked self with sea water in order to break the trail of scent that the creature follows. I scream when the icy water hits my skin. A searing fire grips my ankles and runs up my calves. The sky above opens, and a deluge of rain, as cold as the ocean, falls. I find an abandoned fire pit and force my hands into the wet ash that lines the bottom. Black coats my hands, and I draw two lines on each cheek, like a warrior. With twigs and handfuls of moss I try to build a new fire, but the rain beats all my efforts down. I take a large stick and dance around the dead fire like some sort of shaman, a man of medicine with extraordinary vision, a seer. He told me I was special. That I would be a man of knowledge and of greatness. I fall onto the sand and then get up and start to run. The bare soles of my feet thicken with each step. My foot strikes something hard. I search in the sand and find a handgun. Is this some sort of apparition? I pick the gun up and point it out to the open sea, pull the trigger, and nothing happens. I find a length of rope tangled in a washed up tree root and tie the gun across my chest, like a savage, like a lost boy.

When the sun breaks over the horizon, I raise my arms and kowtow to the sun gods, who have bathed us again with light for one last day. I sit in trance to the beauty and ferocity of the sea. I scream at it and throw rocks until I run what's left of the day's light away to another hemisphere. Even the light itself should fear me. Only the dark that now descends can bring clarity. Then I think of Fern. Beautiful perfect Fern, and I wonder if she has been the true demon all this time. Of course the devil would remake itself into the most tantalizing female form. Of course he would.

I race up to the cliffs, go back to my watchtower where I can survey the land. With my spyglass I study the terrain and spot two human shapes. I yell out to them, "Who are you?" But the wind steals the words from my mouth. "Who are you?" I yell once again, but the sound is pulled out to sea. Filtered through sheets of rain, the clouds, black, and thick, block out the night sky. I climb down and stalk toward them, through the forest. The mossy earth under my feet is slick with rain. I belly crawl onto a rise, and there they are locked in an embrace. I hold my gun out and crawl closer. Are they demons or an apparition? As I near them, I can tell one of the forms is Fern. Fern in the arms of a man. Static consumes me. Who is this man? I lift the gun and take aim through the night curtain of water. There's a bang, and the gun jerks back. Fern screams again and again, and the sound binds itself around my head like a vice.

"Shane," she calls out. "Shane?"

I run to her and study the body on the ground. He's young with smooth skin and thick hair. His eyes closed, his face still. I kneel down beside him and take a closer study of his face. His mouth and nose are so familiar, and then I understand. The man I've shot is my son.

Fern presses her hands against the wound in the middle of his chest. "What have you done?" she screams. "What have you done?"

The sound of her voice pulls me back out of the noise of my brain. "I don't know," I say. "I'm not here." I touch his sodden brow and remember how he came out of his mother with his eyes open. "My son," I say and look at Fern. Her eyes are wide, and I think there's a lack of recognition, a lack of understanding. "This is my son," I say to her.

"What?" she yells, over the wind and rain, and shakes her head. "What?" She covers her face with her hands. Her back, rounded over, convulses. "He said he didn't have a father."

I pull her hands away from her face. "Why are you crying?"

She blinks her eyes, the rain thick on her face.

"Why are you not?" she asks.

—

In the dark, battered by rain and wind, we dig for hours with our hands, sticks, and shells, until we have a hole long enough, and deep enough. All the while the winds get stronger and stronger. Pine needles and branches rain down around us to line the bottom of the grave. We pull Shane by his legs and slide him into the shallow bed. Then we push the pile of unearthed soil over him until he is covered and the ground is even. Fern gathers stones and starts to place them at the head of the grave, but I stop her.

"He should be left unmarked," I say. "We all should."

When I touch Fern's arm, she takes a step back, away from me. There's a hardness in her eyes.

"You shot your own son," she cries and takes another step away.

Rage bursts in my head, and I surrender. Fern is the devil after all. Maybe somewhere deep down I knew it all this time. I aim the gun at her. She yells something at me, but I can't hear it over the wind. Then there's a sound so loud it engulfs us. It's as if the very sky itself and space above with all its planets and stars have crashed down upon us. The earth under me ripples, and for a moment I am aloft, my feet hover the ground. I thud back to earth, covered by a web of tree limbs. A tree trunk over six feet across now lies in the gulf that was between Fern and me. The wind pushes against me, bringing a thick gust of salt air. I imagine that soon the ocean itself will plummet from the heavens.

CHARLES

The forest has come alive and wants to strip me of all my work. I grab blankets and rope and attempt to cover my canvas. We must get out of here if we're to survive. I'll leave these fools, and get my art to a safe place. The wind pulls at the wall boards. It's as if the whole hovel has begun to breathe and at any moment might burst apart like a bloated corpse. With duct tape, I try to secure the blankets around the canvas. Pieces of the roof begin to rattle. A sheet of corrugated metal is sucked up into the night. Rain pours in. I drag my canvas out into the forest and lean it against the base of a thick cedar. With rope and twine, I tie the canvas to the trunk. Sticks, branches, and pinecones rain down all around me. A piece of the hovel's wall is pulled away by the wind. Rain soaked shingles whip about through the air like razor blades. A fishing net that had decorated the exterior of the hovel is now tangled in the branches of a tree, high up in the air. I continue to run rope around the trunk and the painting.

Wind screams in my ears, and rain lashes first east and then south. I fall in the mud that has turned deep at my feet. I could take my painting, strap it to my back, and head for the road. With my masterpiece, I won't return to this sodden nightmare. I'll leave these wretched souls to their own fate. In haste, I free my painting and hoist it onto my back, threading my arms through the supports. I start to take the trail toward the road, but the pathway becomes indistinguishable to everything else, the ground a mat of branches.

Out of nowhere there's a crushing weight on my back. There are blows to my sides. With all my strength I rear up and force the weight of my assailant backwards into the trunk of a tree, and then I see it's Roy, naked, covered in mud and sand. A crystal hangs around his neck, and black is smudged across his cheeks. He jumps up and blubbers something about Fern, lost, separated, a tree. He points some dime-store pistol at me as if it's a threat.

"Where have you got her?" he cries.

"I haven't seen your sow," I yell back, over the wind, and push him out of my way.

He lunges at me, and we wrestle in the muck like pigs.

"Where is she?" he hollers.

"How the hell would I know?"

"You're hiding her."

I steady myself, with the awkwardness of the painting on my back, and take a few steps away from Roy. "Keep track of your whore." The rain brings lashes of water straight into my eyes.

Again he points the black barrel at me and pokes it into my chest. "Garth took my paintings," he yells.

"To amuse himself," I yell back. "He would never take your juvenile finger paintings seriously. He toys with you."

Then he freezes and cups a hand to his ear. "Do you hear that?"

I strain to hear what might be in the air but can't make anything out over the howl of the rain and the wind. His mind must be playing tricks. He's a lunatic.

"Yes, it sounds like Fern," I say. "You should go to her."

"It's singing," he says.

"Singing," I say, but I still can't hear anything other than the forest trying to take my life.

I'm convinced Roy only hears the backfiring of his own brain. He appears entranced. I take a step back and then another. I turn and start to run. I must get to the road. I must find a way into town. I must save my masterpiece.

THOMAS

I slip back into my cave and pull the hatch shut; here in my sanctuary I'll weather this storm. I feast on the last of the drugs. In the morning with the dawn of a new year, I'll go cold turkey. Above me there's the crash and bang of wind clawing at our shelter. I try to dull myself and wish just to sleep, but there's a nervous energy coursing through my heart and limbs. Then a voice from above calls out my name. I open the hatch, take a glance out into the darkness, and see Roy, naked and hunched over, a wild look about him.

"I'm here," I call out over the wind.

He sprints over to me, falls to his knees in the mud. "Iris says you turned her away."

"What?" I gasp, unsure I've heard him right.

"Iris," he yells. "I just saw her. She said you didn't want to see her. She wanted to show you her writing."

All his words shatter inside my body. How can this be? I would never turn Iris away. Rain pelts my back as I scramble out of my hole and frantically run out into the woods. "Iris, Iris," I call out until my voice cracks. I climb over broken trees and search hollows between boulders. The wind and driving rain pushes me back and then forces me forward. Falling branches knock me down. I slip and slide in the mud. The woods feel topsy-turvy, and I lose all sense of direction. North, east, west, and south mean nothing. Through the rain comes a whimper, like a wounded animal. I stop and strain to hear if the sound will come again. Then it does, and I run in its direction, fighting back branches and wading through ankle deep pools of water. I get pushed against a tree by the wind and tumble over its roots. The sound takes me down onto the beach.

Waves beat mean and high-up onto the rocks. I follow a narrow strip of sand left between the cliff face and the ocean. A wave pushes me against the rocks, and I grasp for anything solid to keep me from washing out to sea. The wave in its retreat pulls at my legs and knocks me off balance. Then the sound comes again, a cry or a whimper. My sodden hair drips even more water into my eyes, my clothes weigh me down like an anchor, my ears full with the sounds of the angry air. I steady myself against the rocks, and through the wind I'm sure I hear someone cry, "Dad!" I think of that old man who shot himself and how he survived the beaches of Normandy. We all fight our own battles, someone told me once.

When my daughter was ten I took her out in a row boat, into an inlet known to be shallow and sandy. She spotted a moon snail shell on the bottom and asked if I would get it for her.

"What if I drown?" I asked her.

She burst into tears. I was confused. I didn't know what to do. I told her I'd get the shell and not to cry.

"No," she begged. "Don't go. I don't want you to drown."

"Don't worry," I said. "You want the shell, I'll get it for you." I jumped into the water and swam down and grabbed the shell. When I broke the surface, her face was buried in her hands.

"Here," I said and held the shell out for her.

She grabbed the shell and threw it back into the water. "I didn't want it!" she screamed.

Ahead of me, just in the tree line, there's a flash of movement, a sharp flicker of light. I press through waves, rain, and wind to get closer. A person, slight of build, is on a rise of land, standing on something, maybe a stump. A smudge of pink. I wade through a stream, the water rising into a torrent of wood and froth. The silhouette is familiar to me. "Iris," I cry out. The stump wobbles, and she reaches up over a thick branch. I try to focus on the object in her hand. What is she holding? A gust of wind hits her, and her foot slips. For a moment, she teeters back and forth. "IRIS!" I scream. A fear like nothing I've ever felt before rises in my gut, a fear greater than the shadow. I run and run until another wave tosses me into the rocks. Above her, tied to a branch, is a length of rope that leads to a loop held in her hands. "IRIS!"

She slips the loop over her head.

"IRIS! IRIS!" I scream as loudly as I can, but the wind fills my mouth and tries to steal my voice.

She stops and watches me approach her.

"Iris what are you doing?" I cry.

"I came to the hut, and they told me you didn't want to see me."

"No. It's not true."

"Everything from you is a lie."

"It is," I say.

A violent squall pushes against us and then pulls at our limbs. Deep in the forest trees moan and creek; they sound like spirits fighting their way out of limbo.

"Iris," I plead.

Our eyes meet, and I pray for her to say something, the most hurtful things, if she must. I would accept any and all cruelties. I deserve it. But she doesn't speak. We look into each other's eyes, and I see myself. If she sees anything, she keeps it to herself and steps off the stump. My knees buckle and hit the sand beneath me. None of my muscles respond. When the sound of my own screams subside, and my vision returns, Iris is in my arms, the life in her extinguished.

ROY

There's a story I tell to almost every woman I meet. Every woman who spends enough time with me. I cry, hang my head in her lap, and proclaim how the man in the headdress said I would be special, how I would go out into the world and do magnificent things. One day, he said, he would read about my greatness. We were in a small town where everyone overlapped in one way or another, and I would see him outside the liquor store or down on the dock fishing for trout. There were whispers about his cottage on the lake. It was best if one didn't go there. He started to talk to me and tell me stories about logging in the mountains and gave me candy. One day I saw him and he had a bag from the bakery. Cinnamon buns, he said. If I came over he would fry them in butter. So I went.

His place was on stilts and looked out over the quiet end of the lake. There wasn't much inside but an upholstered rocker, a kitchen table, two wood chairs, and an old black and white TV with bunny ears. He told me to sit down at the table, and he took out the buns, sliced them in half, and fried them on the stove in butter. He asked me questions about my family, about my mother. Asked if I knew my dad. I told him my dad lived somewhere else and that I never saw him.

"That must make you sad?" he said.

And I guess it did, although no one had ever asked before.

"My dad wasn't around either," he said. "That must make us a lot alike."

He asked what I liked to do, and I told him, swim in the lake, hang out with my friends, and draw.

"Draw," he said. "You're an artist?"

"I guess," I said.

"Show me your creations."

On the next visit, I brought my drawings, and he pored over them, and told me I had promise, and what a magical person I would be. He placed a slice of apple pie in front of me and let me have one of his cigarettes. He said I was welcome any time. He said we were lost boys.

I liked the sound of that, 'lost boys', like I belonged to no one, least of all my mother.

I would get up in the mornings and think about what he might buy from the bakery that day. He named me Tootles but called me Toot. He said this was my lost boy name. Why, I don't know. It was all stupid, and none of it matters. I was to call him Chief, and he would put on an Indian headdress and chase me.

One night I went home, and the door was locked. Inside there was loud music. I went around to the living room window, and there was my mom. She had on a green dress and was doing a dance. Her hair had partially fallen out of where she had pinned it up. In her hand was a glass full of booze that lazily looped through the air with her stilted dance moves. On the couch, slouched down low, was a guy who worked at the school. I banged on the window. He glanced over at me but didn't move.

The rain started to come down in cold fat drops. I went to the back door and tried the knob, but it too was locked. I banged and banged on the door, but no one came. I ran down the road and sat in the wood shelter of a bus stop. Frozen to the bone, I tried to warm myself by rubbing the sleeves of my wet jean jacket. Then there was Chief in his white Impala. He leaned over the wide seat and opened the passenger side door. I could already taste the pies or cakes he might have. I hadn't eaten all day.

It was all Chief's fault. If it wasn't for him, I would never have thought that I might be special. That I could become something, worth anything to anybody. I cried this to Fern. "If it wasn't for him," I said.

"Who cares," she said, "what some pedophile thought?"

When Fern says shit like that, it makes me so fucking mad, I could smash her head in.

"He's not," I yelled. "He's not."

And I run, and run, down the road, out onto the wharf, and into the lake. The water rushes up quickly over my head. All the world is muffled. My pulse beats in my ears, and I scream until the water fills my mouth, fills my nose. My chest fights for air. All my muscles burn. Then I wake, the scream still on my lips and my hands in tight fists. I gasp for air, the taste of lake in my mouth. A vision of my son comes to me in the form of an angel. His baby face against my ear. At first I can't hear what he says. I want to so bad. I believe he has some grand question to ask. But it's gibberish that comes out of his mouth. I fight against the water that weighs down my tongue and finally say, "What is it boy? What do you want to know?"

He floats back, and with clear and precise words he says, "I hate you."

—

I wake up when my shoulder slams into the plywood wall of the watchtower. The wind through the forest below me is a terrifying roar. Trees pulled and pushed side to side. I climb down, needing to go back to the spot where I shot my son. Is it plausible that it was just a dream or a hallucination? Wind pulls from above and tries to suck me into the sky. The forest threatens to explode around me, trees creak, and bang. I search for the spot where I buried my son. Frantic, I run from tree to tree and remember how once I was told that when people are lost they will continually go in circles. I flail about, running north, and then south. Branches rain down around me. So much water is in the air I fear a tsunami. The grave is unmarked, and I curse Fern. I should have let her place the stones down. Remember never to interfere with the harmless intentions of a woman. I climb up over rocks and down into gullies and come to a place where I'm sure my son lies, but the earth looks unbroken.

CHARLES

I trip over a tree root obscured by the mud and water that covers the forest floor, and twist my ankle. On the ground, wet and miserable, I pull myself to partial shelter under a crosshatch of tree trunks, fallen across the trail. I don't know what my daughters want from me. No wonder they have no men, with their sour demeanours and unsmiling faces. What have they to complain about? Prosperity and peace have been the foundation of their existences. They're free to do whatever they want. Why they come and mope around me I cannot fathom. Let them live my life for a day and they would gladly go back to their own.

I'm of the 'silent generation'. Silent because we didn't speak up, didn't use our voices in the political arena. But I know why we were silent. We were crushed under the weight of death, under households that became shrines to those lost, those of the greatest generation. How could we compete? How can you compete with the ghost of a man who was so perfect that all he did in life and death grew to the stature of sainthood? Those in the throes of mourning saints cannot be bothered with whatever minor frivolities mere mortals accomplish. A home darkened by a saint has no room or time for other's disparate thoughts.

In Paris, I lived like a vagrant, loitered in cafés, dance halls, and the dingy narrow streets. All the time haunted by the fucking saint, dead in the ground of Dieppe, a few hours west. It was as if every cobblestone, brick, and doorway was haunted by him, mon cher frère. Even though only his corpse ever touched the shores of this country. France was no more than a flash for him out the window of a Spitfire.

I bought a train ticket to Dieppe to view his grave, but with the ticket in my pocket I wandered into a bar and didn't leave until they pushed me out into the street some time during the night. I rambled through the dark streets and sang Bing Crosby tunes to the shuttered windows and gas lamps. I woke, slumped in a doorway, took one glance at the bleak Parisian sky, and knew I had to get out of the country; there was nothing in France for me. I would abandon the ghost I was chasing. My father once said, Europe is a cemetery and nothing more.

ROY

All around me, trees snap and crash to the forest floor. I run back to the shack, now only three walls and a collapsed roof. I rifle through my meagre possessions until I find what I search for. Under a pile of brushes and tubes of oil paint is a wallet-sized photograph of my son as an infant. I'm struck by how this infant's face is like a puff of smoke that has dissipated into time and space, into something I barely understand. What is a baby anyway but something that becomes unrecognizable, something that ceases to exist moments after the photo is taken? If it weren't for the writing on the back, "Shane, 2 months," I wouldn't even be sure this image had been my child at all.

As I leave the shack, I grab a bundle of feathers and stab them into my braids, tight to the scalp. I run with the photograph clenched in my fist, protected from the sheets of rain, to the watchtower and start to climb. The thick trunk, pushed by the wind, leans to one side and then rocks back to the other when the gust relents. Several times my feet slide across the wet boards, and for a moment, I hang out over the forest floor like a bed sheet on a clothes line. I gain purchase once again, and climb, ignoring the rain on my face and body. The forest around me wails.

In the crow's nest, I'm tossed from side to side as the tree is assaulted by gales carrying the thick scent and cold of the ocean. If I was a real lost boy, I'd brandish my sword at the storm and tell it to go away, not to bother us anymore. With sodden twigs and strips of cloth I build a fire in a metal bucket. Fire is an amazing thing, bright and hot. Like the fire that burns at the centre of my chest. I wait till the fire fills the bucket, and I take out a single razor blade. I pull one braid taut, and near the scalp, I press the sharp edge into the hair. The blade slices through each strand and leaves the plait limp in my hand. I toss it into the fire and watch the fibres burst with flame and then curl and dance. I slice through the other braid and release it too, to the fire. The fire, like every fire, is hungry and wants more. I pick up an eagle feather and hold it together with the photograph of my son. My son who is dead, the son I killed. I'm a man between a dead father and a dead son, bookended by death. I drop the feather into the fire, and the flames sizzle. The fire eats each barb like a hungry ghost.

The heat on my face is so hot, I'm certain blisters will begin to form. It might be the best thing I've ever felt. It might be the first thing I've ever felt. What would the man in the headdress say? Come sit down. I have cinnamon buns. Come give me a hug. The fingers of the fire reach out for the photograph of Shane. There's a cabin on the lake that all the kids in town say you shouldn't go to, that you should stay away from. The fire burns my hands, and then there's a crack sound that ricochets through the treetops like the blast of a cannon, so loud I can't tell in which direction it originates. Could it be Captain Hook's *Sea Devil* offshore? I stand up and feel the boards beneath me give way. An intense roar—like the very earth itself cracking open— overwhelms the night. For a moment my body hangs in space, blackness above, and blackness below. My being is weightless before gravity pushes me to the forest floor.

THOMAS

The shock of the cold Pacific water is like so many other shocks in life. The kind of shocks that slam the air out of your body and fill you with unending pain. The pain overwhelms, numbs you, takes all the strength out of your limbs. It robs you of your will to fight, until you go still, and sink.

When I was a boy I was raped by a man I called the shadow. The same man on several occasions. I always wonder what he saw in me? Why he chose me? Did he see someone who was willing? Did he see someone he could take advantage of? Over and over I ask these questions. Can people tell what happened when they look at me? Like the day I saw everything in the eyes of that young boy with the blonde hair.

I take my shoes and socks off and set my feet on the cold wet sand. The surf is high and crashes into the surrounding rock, filling my head with its symphony. I step into the water and push forward. My legs scream, and then my hips, and torso. Before I am lifted from the land the numbness has already set in. I swim. Waves carry me up and then down into gullies where only walls of water surround me. I swim until I feel the grasp of the ocean pull at my legs, and I let go.

CHARLES

I fight my way through broken branches that threaten to remove my head. The weight of my masterpiece, on my back, grows ever heavier. I tell myself that the ground is still solid under my feet, even though it doesn't feel so. The earth has come alive. Any moment the ground will heave open and swallow us all. This will be an epic story, told to a rapt crowd at the opening of my next show. The wild man of the coast, how he fought through the storm of the century to save his painting. Surely the prices of my work will skyrocket. My daughters too will all be there, because they're an integral part of this tale. Perhaps their recollections of tonight will be even more fantastical than my own. Maybe they'll even sing. Who knew this was a talent they shared, the Tindal Girls.

Trees splinter and topple in every direction. Great gusts of wind push me forward and then want to lift me up into the air. I must be greater and stronger than any common man. I must be an animal to tear through the underbrush and force my way out of this wet dark hell. I must be a soldier and blast my way through the enemy.

Up ahead, an eerie light glows in the underbrush. Perhaps some type of illusion or luminescence. The glow grows stronger the closer I get. Then I realize it's one of my daughters, in her white gown. When I get very close, I can tell it's Cedar. She's on her knees and appears to sob into her hands. She's my youngest and favourite. Perhaps she'll help her old father get out of the woods.

I sit on a spongy log beside her, disgusted with my sodden state. I must appear a real ghoul. Cedar's back heaves up and down, the nobs of her spine pressing into her wet robe. Her delicate hands cover her face.

"I will name the painting, *Sombrio*," I call out over the wind. "It will be the crown jewel at my next opening." I remain silent for a moment to provide Cedar a chance to comment, but she doesn't. "The tale of our adventure here will be a fortuitous addition to my narrative, much like the years I lived in Europe, and then in boats of various forms. It will be legendary, just like the stories of Rimbaud or Hemingway."

Cedar sits up and rests her hands on the plump flesh above her knees. "Rimbaud and Hemingway were mentally ill," she sputters against the rain.

Her sisters have really poisoned her. I hold Miranda to account for this. "The hovel has been destroyed," I yell. "The roof got torn away into the treetops." Cedar's face is frightful and pale with blue and black under her eyes. "Jesus, you look awful," I tell her.

"You say that so often," she cries.

I don't know what she's going on about, but I think to mention that I'm on my way to the road and that she should help me get there.

"What if genius could only be cast upon those who didn't break their children?" she yells over the gusts that pummel us.

What is this nonsense? It's as if some demon has taken her. She opens her mouth wide, bares her teeth like a statue of a woman about to scream. Her mouth opens even wider, and I think of a serpent about to unhinge its jaw and swallow me whole. I search the surroundings for something to defend myself with; I may have to strike her. Then I hear them again, their blasted voices, out there somewhere in the dark. *It Ain't Me, Babe*, sung slow like a dirge over the sounds of the storm. Cedar sits up, then gets to her feet.

"Cedar," I yell. "Show your pa to the road."

"Ruined," she cries out loud, but it seems to be to herself. Then she turns and jolts away like a banshee. She scrambles over broken trees and fades into the dark, until the last of her white gown is lost. I forgot to ask if she thought I was right about my legacy and the increased value of my paintings. Still the signing continues unabated.

I must get out of the woods and start again to hike in the direction of the road. The singing grows louder, as if I'm moving closer to it rather than further away. It's a trap, I'm sure, and I change direction. I beat back branches that want to catch on my masterpiece. The wind's howl and the singing whip together. I throw my palms against my ears. I should have reached the road by now. When I take in my surroundings, it appears I'm in the exact same spot where I spoke with Cedar. How can this be? Those women have bewitched the forest and caused me to lose my way. The winds have grown in strength, to a scream, and I decide to head back to what's left of the hovel, but that too seems impossible. I recognize nothing. My masterpiece grows steadily heavier.

Ahead of me, an apparition, three shapes cloaked in white. I know they're my daughters.

"Help your pa," I call out to them. "Take me back to the hovel."

They sway and remain mute, shimmery, otherworldly spooks.

Blue, bows her head and appears to sob, then Miranda does the same, and then Cedar.

"Cedar, help your pa," I yell. "Cedar!"

The sound of their cries grows in intensity until it overtakes the wind and the groans of trees that rub and knock against each other. The cries grow and grow until they swirl around me like a tornado, until I'm unsure if the sound is the earth about to open up and swallow me.

"Why do you treat your pa like this?" I yell. With each step I take toward them, they seem to fall further away.

I painted pictures of them when they were infants, with their fat limbs, and open mouths, always full of want and need. I'd tell their mothers to take them away. An infant is like an enraged albatross in an art studio; they bash into things, squawk, and shit everywhere. The window must be opened for their exit and peace. Their mothers were the window. When I looked at their little faces, I felt like an empty book. There were no words to pull out for their amusement.

I stumble forward. The rain beats me back, but still I try to reach them. My canvas catches the wind like a sail. I climb over a fallen tree, the root ball lifted high into the air, and slip on the wet bark, landing hard on the ground. My palm is punctured by a stick. A bolt of pain blasts into my elbow. Fireworks explode in my chest. I stare at my hand, my paint brush hand. I grab the stick and pull it from the flesh. With the stick held high, I howl into the wet and black night. My punctured palm throbs, and I press it to my chest.

"Help your pa!" I scream.

The girls appear high in the trees, jerked back and forth with the wind. Could my brain be playing tricks on me? Is it just the clouds and sky? They begin to move further away and I stumble forward to follow them. I'm sure they'll lead me to safety. "Help your pa!" I scream again, reaching out to them with my bloody hand. Blood runs down my arm and stains my waterlogged garments. The girls move through the branches and out into a clearing. Rain pelts my face and tries to push me backward, but I must follow them. The dirt beneath me softens, my feet slip on mud, and suddenly I feel light. A cold blast presses against me, then changes course, catching on the canvas, and sucks me out into the open. I reach and cry to my daughters. The forest floor no longer under me, I begin to fall, and fall, and fall, into the dark, toward the beach below. My ears fill with the crash of the surf and the scream of the wind. I search the sky for my daughters, but they are no longer there. I glimpse their broken bodies mixed with the ocean, rock, and sand as I fall toward them.

The End

ABOUT THE AUTHOR

Rhonda Waterfall studied Sales and Marketing at The Sauder School of Business at the University of British Columbia and Creative Writing at The Writer's Studio at Simon Fraser University, where she was mentored by Stephen Osborne. For many years she worked in ad agencies directing print production and managing creatives and the creative process. For a time she lived in Zimbabwe and worked for the Zimbabwe Book Development Council, where she was involved in creating *The Zimbabwean Book Directory* and event planning for the Zimbabwe International Book Fair. She has had fiction and non-fiction published in several literary journals along with the novel, *The Strait of Anian* (Now or Never Publishing) and a short story collection, *The Only Thing I Have* (Arsenal Pulp Press). She was born in what is now the ghost town of Ocean Falls on the west coast of Canada and currently lives in Toronto.